RACER

A Hamster's Tale

Front Cover Illustration by
Robb from Pro Service from Romania

Back Cover Illustration by Vicki Friedman
http://inspirangels.com/

ISBN: 978-1503211476

Disclaimer

All characters are fictional and not meant to portray any real person, living or dead. Except for the cat, the cat is real. All towns, roads and areas mentioned are real, but not all of them are on the map.

Warning # 1

This book contains severe silliness.

Warning # 2

There will be a quiz at the end, so pay attention.

Prologue

Once upon a time, in a green and beautiful land, there lived an evil scientist and he had a pet hamster. His name was Racer. The hamster, that is. Not that it's important, just in case you wanted to know.

Chapter 1

Racer ran round and round, round and round, round and round, flying down the pathway to heaven. At least, that's the way he saw it. To anyone else it looked like a hamster's exercise wheel, but to Racer it was his outlet for stress. It's not easy being the beloved pet of a mad scientist.

Lefter wandered into the room looking around for a clue as to why he was there. He was sure there was something he was supposed to be doing, but he couldn't remember what.

But memory lapse wasn't what Lefter was known for. Lefter had a genetic quirk that urged him to turn to the left whenever he was going somewhere. Lefter wasn't his real name, of course. No one could remember what his original name was. He was just Lefter. He spent a lot of his life going in circles.

Finally, Lefter's eyes landed on the box of hamster food and he remembered, *Feed Racer*! That's what Dr. Cutter had told him to do. Dr. Cutter was Lefter's uncle and he had no patience for his nephew's mistakes or anyone else's.

Lefter filled Racer's food dish, and gave him fresh water and a piece of advice: "Take a break pal. You're going to wear yourself out on that thing."

Racer understood him, but he couldn't stop. He had a genetic quirk too, and that was to run in circles for hours on end. He had what Dr. Cutter called 'the round and round gene.' When other hamsters would knock off for a nap and a smoke, Racer would keep on going. Among the other hamsters he was known as something of an oddball.

Across the room, large golden eyes watched the cage on the counter. Squeaker Cat had waited a long time to get her claws on that uppity good-for-nothing rodent. Sooner or later someone was going to make a mistake and leave that cage door open; she could wait. She settled herself down into her basket where she could keep an eye on the cage and purred quietly to herself.

In another part of the building, Dr. Helga Lindstrom and Dr. Linda Lapp slumped their shoulders and stared at each other. Ever since their attempt to clone Alan

Greenspan had failed, their stock had fallen in their boss's eyes.

"I don't know what's wrong with those Greenspan cells, Helga," complained Dr. Linda. "Why can't they multiply in a regular sequence like ordinary cells? Is that too much to ask? After all, all those other people we cloned turned out fine."

"It's not that they can't multiply," replied Dr. Helga. "They don't want to; they're using some obscure formula no one else can understand. Not surprising, considering the source. But what about us? If we get the axe, can we take some of this stuff with us? Anthrax, plague, ricin; what do you think would look good on a resume?" They shuffled their lab notes and checked the wall clock for lunchtime.

"Come on, Linda, if we get sacked, we can at least do it on a full stomach. I hear it's chicken pot pie today." Dr. Linda straightened up and smiled. Maybe there was hope after all.

Dr. Cutter, the head of Plastic Genetics Laboratory, had been scowling at them in the hallway lately and rumors of layoffs and budget cuts had been flying faster than you could blink. 'Racer Rumors,' they were called. Dr. Cutter would be seen petting and talking to his pet hamster and afterwards would be heard talking aloud to himself about "incompetent associates" and "things around here have to change."

No one was sure if the hamster was giving suggestions to his owner or not; however, no one held any grudges against Racer. He was a friendly, outgoing hamster and the lab staff liked him.

Located in the beautiful river hills of Lancaster County, the Plastic Genetics Laboratory, LLC, was cutting-edge medical technology.

Dr. Cutter, despite his name, was not a surgeon. No! No cut-and-stitch monsters would be coming out of this laboratory. Dr. Cutter was a geneticist. The mixing and matching of DNA from far and wide was his magic wand, his alchemy.

Okay, so the kudzu-piranha creature hadn't worked out so well. After it escaped from the lab and eaten a small child, there was no end of trouble hushing the incident up.

But Dr. Cutter didn't allow himself to be deterred by setbacks. There was always another day, always another pairing to try – especially when he had customers with deep pockets to fund his work. Governments, too, were a steady source of income. Foreign or domestic, Dr. Cutter didn't care. His mission statement was: Ethics are for sissies!

Chapter 2

At the corner of Park Avenue and East 41st Street, Manhattan, in a stuffy, opulent study, business leaders were doing what business leaders do best: drinking, smoking and plotting how to transfer money from your pocket to theirs. The Tobacco Overlords, American Division (T.O.A.D.) meeting had ended and joy had not been dispensed. No matter how you tried to explain it or disguise it, sales were down. Their archenemy, the American Lung Association, was having great success helping people quit smoking. Their latest announcement was a contest to create a vaccine against nicotine.

Burlington Chesterfield leaned back in his chair and eyed his companions with no enthusiasm. They were good enough for drinking and poker parties, but they had no vision, no creativity, he thought.

"It's not like the old days, Barclay," intoned Chesterfield. "We can't go around putting our hands into people's pockets and taking money blatantly like the I.R.S. That would be sweet. What a set-up those guys have! We need something new, Barclay, something so subtle people won't even realize they're being robbed. No, we have to come up with a new angle."

Barclay frowned with unaccustomed mental effort. "What about using the candy cigarettes idea, with some real cigarettes mixed in?" he asked. "We could give away free samples at kindergartens, day-care centers and playgrounds. It's amazing how many parents don't notice what their kids are doing."

"We tried that five years ago and the ALA jumped all over us. We need to move into an area they aren't watching. I mean, people are going to die anyway, why shouldn't they have a nice smoke while they're doing it?" He drummed his fingers on the table and surveyed the blank I-don't-have-any-ideas faces turned toward him. He sighed; it looked like he was going to have to think up of a new tactic to pull the company out of its slump.

But he didn't feel good, not at all. A dull pressure started forming around his heart, growing in intensity. He tried to push the tingling pain out of his mind. Suddenly he grasped his heart, lurching forward onto the long mahogany table with a loud, gasping groan. "No! No! Not again," he begged an unknown power. "Why? Why? We only want to make money, is that a crime?"

"Chesterfield, what's wrong? Should I call an ambulance?" Barclay looked anxiously at his C.E.O. and froze in indecision. Should he reach for the phone or seize his chance and finish the old buzzard off? But Barclay hesitated a little too long and Burlington pulled himself back into his chair and forced his features into a mask of calm control.

"No, no, it's not a heart attack, another person just quit smoking! It always gets to me like that. What are we going to do? If these blasted health people convince the public that tobacco's bad for them, we're goners! Call the lawyers! Ever since we tried that marketing campaign aimed at kids, we need to be careful. Cryin' shame too; that was going so well."

It is at this point, if there are any tobacco lawyers reading this, that they should put down their swords and their cell phones and go back to doing whatever it is that tobacco lawyers do all day long. Possibly working to make the world a better place.

Chapter 3

Squeaker Cat watched as her human, Dr. Linda frowned over her work. Dr. Linda hadn't been happy lately and Squeaker was concerned. Squeaker considered it her job to help Dr. Linda relax and she tried everything she could think of to ease the strain. She kept telling her about the Cat's Credo: 'If it doesn't involve tuna, it's not really important.' But it was an idea humans couldn't seem to grasp.

Dr. Linda was worried about losing her job and also worried about keeping her job. She needed the money to support her sick mother, but, working for an evil scientist! President Bramble's disastrous economic policies had made a hash out of the country and forced her into this desperate choice. And now look what she was working on!

"How about making a tuna-flavored hamster?" Squeaker coaxed her. "That would be tasty. Nothing evil about that!"

"You hush," she replied. "As if I don't have enough work on my plate. And leave Racer alone. If you kill him, we'll be out on the street so fast you won't have time to shed another hair."

Squeaker bit her tongue and bided her time. Deep jealousy filled the plump little tortoise-shell cat. She was loved by Dr. Linda and petted by some of the staff, but she didn't get the attention that blasted hamster did. What did people see in him? She settled back and tried to devise a plot to discredit Racer and increase her own popularity. She had no idea how to do this, but maybe she could watch some human politicians on TV and pick up a few pointers.

Dr. Linda looked down at her chart and chewed on her lip. What a waste of time it was to be trying to make cows that produced milk with nicotine in it. What she really wanted to be working on was making a vaccine against nicotine.

She saw Lefter going out for his regular cigarette breaks and it made her sad and worried. She had a secret liking for Lefter and fretted that the cigarettes were ruining his health. Just then, Lefter drifted into the room with his usual puzzled look. He found that a puzzled look deflected work.

"Lefter, were you smoking again?" Dr. Linda charged him. "I wish you wouldn't, it's so bad for you. That cough you've had all winter is getting worse."

Lefter's heart swelled with a secret joy at these words. He had a crush on Dr. Linda for a long time, but had never dared to say it. He fiddled with the clipboard in his hand while he worked up the courage to say something, anything.

"Well Miss Dr., I'll quit if you want me to. I'd do anything for you." Lefter looked at her hopefully, his long thin face looking for a crumb of encouragement.

"Oh, Lefter, it's not that easy" Dr. Linda sighed. "You need to get into a program, get a prescription and join a support group. Quitting is a long, hard fight," she said sympathetically.

"I...I...I can too quit, just you wait and see," he protested. "Just you wait and see." Lefter straightened his spine and left the room with a determined look. This was the first time Dr. Linda had said she'd cared about him and he was going to show her how much it meant to him. Lion-like feelings started rumbling within him. I'll show her! Just you wait and see. I might not be a genius like Uncle Dr. Cutter, but I can do it!

Lefter had not been showered with brains by the fates, but he had a great deal of determination and iron will once he found focus and inspiration. A new sun was dawning on Lefter's life and he wasn't about to waste it.

He went to the nearest trashcan, pulled out his cigarettes and tossed them in. Next went the lighter and then the cigarette coupons; there, that was that.

A junior lackey scientist watched from across the lab and laughed snidely. "Quitting, Lefter? It's not that easy. I don't know why people think they can do it like that. You'd have a better chance of winning the lottery." Lefter dared to glare at him and walked away to ponder his next move.

It turned out there wasn't a next move for Lefter to make. It was three months later and he hadn't touched a cigarette since that day. Not only hadn't he smoked, he hadn't wanted to smoke. No cravings, no withdrawal symptoms, nothing. Lefter had no explanation for it and Dr. Linda was incredulous.

"I can't believe it, Lefter, how can that be? People just don't do that! It's not normal, it's not human." Lefter looked at her reproachfully, what did she mean, not human? Lefter was a little touchy on the subject since many of the scientists often mistook him for a larger sort of lab rat. He had hoped so hard to please her and now she doubted him.

"I don't know how I did it Miss Dr., I just made up my mind and did it. Maybe it's in my genes; my mother was the same way." Dr. Linda paused and looked at him thoughtfully. Could it be true? Could Lefter have the key to the nicotine vaccine she was looking for? She approached him slowly, so as not to frighten him and said "Lefter, I want you to do me a favor."

Chapter 4

Back on Park Avenue, tobacco lawyer Nelson Hambright shuffled his papers nervously and chewed on the inside of his cheek. He'd been summoned by the big boss to go over the new campaign with a fine-tooth comb and he was worried. Heads had rolled over the "Ciggies for Kiddies" campaign. Who could have foreseen that parents and the media would object to children smoking? The world was a crazy place.

He was fond of his head on his shoulders and intended to keep it right where it was. His big presentation to the board of directors was in five minutes and his nerves were jumping like grasshoppers in a frying pan.

He longed desperately for a cigarette, but no, he had promised himself he wouldn't. Nelson found himself in the peculiar position of not being able to smoke in a company that allowed smoking; even encouraged it right in the building. There were no huddled masses outside on the sidewalk getting their fix at this company. He could very easily walk over to the smoking lounge and light up. Heck, he could even smoke during the board meeting if he wanted to. The state of New York had banned all indoor smoking, but anyone who called himself a tobacco overlord wasn't about to listen to any puny state government.

But Nelson was in a tight spot. A chance encounter with a shapely young woman who worked for the American Lung Association had turned his world upside down. Walking downtown one day, a furious downpour drove him to seek shelter in the nearest doorway. Fate made it the doorway of the ALA and Fate sank the knife and gave it a good twist in the shape of Doreen.

She had softly curling brown hair, dreamy blue eyes and a figure to make any man alive weak in the knees – Nelson didn't have a chance. She gathered him in from the storm, dried off his glasses and fed him organic cookies and herbal tea. "Poor thing, you'll catch your death of cold out there," she cooed. Nelson had never heard sweeter words.

That wasn't the problem. The problem was that she made him sit through a screening of *Tobacco, Death's Right Hand Man*. That film and Doreen's lovely face opened Nelson's eyes to a reality he couldn't deny. He was desperately in love; and to save his life and win fair lady, he needed to quit smoking.

How could he do it? He couldn't ask anybody at work. Not only wouldn't they know how, they would rat him out and old Chessie would sack him. No, he had to be sly about it. Nelson summoned dormant brain cells out of retirement and ordered them to report front and center.

Chapter 5

Lab 3C sat at the sunny corner of Plastic Genetics Lab's main building. The windows wrapped around the corner of the room, providing a spectacular view of the Susquehanna River. It was the best lab at the company and of course Dr. Cutter had pegged it out for himself. 'The best for the best,' he would tell others.

Ever since he'd been tossed out of the World Stem Cell Hub for unethical dealings, he was a little touchy about his reputation. He'd crossed killer bees with dragonflies, and created a very successful killing machine with a three-foot wingspan for a third world dictator. They were a great success, but the U.N. and human rights groups had raised a fuss about it, and so they were destroyed. What a bunch of crybabies!

Dr. Cutter and Dr. Helga were unpacking a new shipment of material one morning. "Now, Dr. Helga, here's what I want you to start working on," started Dr. Cutter. "We managed to get genetic samples from Congress, Penndot and several state and local politicians; don't ask how, let's just say money talks.

17

This gives us a wide array of styles and varieties of stupidity to study. Most people don't realize that stupidity is a natural force, like gravity. Examples of stupidity have been found throughout history, in all civilizations, and it doesn't show any signs of running low. It's an inexhaustible source of energy, a perpetual motion machine if only we could learn how to harness it."

"What about bungee jumpers?" Dr. Helga asked, "Or those young people with multiple facial piercings? There seem to be more and more of them around, maybe stupidity is contagious, like the flu."

"If it is, we need to hurry and be the first ones to make something useful out of it; it's a gold mine waiting to be tapped." Dr. Cutter paused and indulged in a favorite daydream: he would corner the energy market and become an overlord himself.

He pictured himself at his monthly poker game with the other overlords, crooked government agents and cabal leaders. "By the way boys, I've cornered the energy market, better be nice to me from now on." It gave him a warm, fuzzy glow of power. They'd never try to slip an extra ace in on him again!

Behind his back, Dr. Helga looked at him sourly. She had weighed herself this morning and the scale had not been kind. Gained another two pounds! Was there no justice? She and Dr. Linda had dieted and exercised for years to trim their figures, and there was no lasting effect.

To add insult to injury, there was Lefter. Just yesterday she watched Lefter wolf down yet another

18

cheese steak, onion rings and milkshake meal. Lefter was one of those tall, skinny men who ate like a horse, didn't exercise and never gained weight.

It galled Dr. Linda and she didn't have an outlet for her frustration and feelings of injustice. She'd been working on weight loss ideas at the lab behind Dr. Cutter's back for some time now. But her experiments and research had only been similar to other doctors' with the same temporary, disappointing results.

She needed inspiration; she needed genius and it was no use asking Dr. Cutter. He considered it women's problem and wouldn't waste his time on it. Maybe she should ask Racer. That hamster had come up with more than one good idea; like latte coffee shops and air bags for cars. He also came up with the idea for the 'Mad Scientist Starter Kit for Children' (coupon included for human brain). It was wildly successful and provided the funding that built the Plastic Genetics Laboratory. For a hamster that seldom got out into the world, he had an amazing interest in it.

Dr. Cutter opened Racer's cage and gently lifted him out. Racer was probably the only living thing Dr. Cutter cared about. No one was sure where Dr. Cutter had come from or what his background was. There were rumors that he was a genetic experiment gone wrong, a genius created to lead humanity into a golden age that instead had turned to the dark side, but no one was brave enough to ask him.

He stroked the hamster gently, slowly tracing the diagonal silver streak on the animal's side, a racing stripe that had given him his name. Fate had played a

19

joke on the two of them by pairing the naturally good hamster with the naturally evil scientist.

Racer snuggled up against him, enjoying the attention. Racer knew that Dr. Cutter was evil, but he loved him anyway. From the ancients mists of history there had always been a special bond between a man and his hamster and Racer was not about to let his human down.

"Can't you keep that cat away from me? It gives me the willies when she stares at me like that," pleaded Racer. "She's up to no good, I'm sure of it."

"I'll do what I can, Racer, but I need Dr. Linda and if I make her get rid of her pet, she'll be a wreck and get nothing done. Maybe I can slip some sedatives into the cat food. I need a new idea Racer, one that will make people sit up and take notice. Something that will make my name go down in history and bring in lots of money. Hamster food doesn't grow on trees, you know."

Racer thought furiously, but came up with nothing; sometimes ideas came and sometimes they didn't. "How about working on Lefter? Maybe that left-hand turn gene of his could be good for something."

"Well, I don't know, he's pretty useless. Open up your mouth and let me take a cheek swab from you. Maybe all your running energy can be tapped. I'll play around with it and see what happens."

"Lefter!" he barked, "Take these specimens down to Dr. Baker. Stop! Wait, come here a minute; I want to take a cheek swab from you."

Lefter approached reluctantly. It's not that cheek swabs hurt; he just didn't like the idea of his genes in the hands of evil. Lefter wasn't religious by nature, but he had seen many of the freaks that had come out of the lab and he instinctively distrusted the whole idea of genetics.

"Come on, come on, I don't have all day. I don't know why I keep you around. If I hadn't promised my dying sister to look after you, I don't know where you'd be."

"You killed my mother, Uncle Dr.! That gene therapy you gave her for toe-cramp syndrome did her in, I'm sure of it." These were daring words for Lefter. Usually he did whatever Dr. Cutter told him to do and tried to stay out of the way. But love was stirring in Lefter, bringing up from the depths of his being boldness and courage that had long gone unused.

"Never mind about that, Lefter; some things don't work out the way you plan. You just do what you're told and you'll always have a job here. Remember Lefter, I'm a genius and you're not."

"Yes, Uncle Dr.," Lefter sighed. He looked down and scuffed the floor with his foot. He wanted to make a snappy comeback, but that skill had never been his. In the break room he remembered seeing a catalog from HACC that advertised a class in Snippy Sarcasm, Snappy Comebacks and Rapid Retorts every Tuesday night; maybe that was just the thing he needed.

He promised himself to find that catalog and develop new skills in his life. Lefter exited the room with his new plan in mind, followed by Dr. Cutter. Dr. Helga saw her chance. She walked over to Racer's cage and looked down at the golden rodent.

"Racer," she hissed, "Help me. Dr. Linda and I have tried everything to lose weight. None of my experiments have worked out, and I don't know what to try next."

Racer sat up and gave her his full attention. He liked Dr. Helga and although he was puzzled by humans' quest for slimness, he was ready to help her if he could. "Maybe you're approaching it from the wrong angle," he said. "Instead of studying fat people, maybe you should study people who are naturally skinny, like Lefter."

Now, Racer had not meant any harm to Lefter with this suggestion, but as happens so often, after words leave one's mouth, they take on a life of their own and sometimes make a quick left turn. No pun intended.

Dr. Helga's eyes narrowed in concentration as she reviewed her resources. Plastic Genetics wasn't equipped with an operating theater; it wasn't that kind of laboratory; so cutting someone up wasn't going to be easy. Dr. Helga wasn't originally a geneticist, she was a surgeon; but after that unpleasant incident in California, she had to change her name and seek work in another field.

"People just don't appreciate the need for medical experiments," she fumed to herself. That patient didn't understand that she was writing a page in medical history when Dr. Helga had put eyes in the back of her head. No appreciation at all.

Dr. Helga sighed, and indulged in a moment of self-pity. Then she shook herself and turned her attention back to the problem at hand. How was she going to extract Lefter's skinny secret? She noticed that Lefter shied away from her, but maybe he would trust Dr. Linda. She made a mental note to bring the conversation around to Lefter when she next talked to her.

Chapter 6

Dr. Cutter took the two samples he collected to his workstation and started processing them. He tried this and he tried that: nothing. He tried all ten standard combinations in chapter one of the *Advanced Mad Scientist's Manual* (3rd edition) and nothing was working out. No promising leads presented themselves, no profitable traits jumped up and waved to catch his attention.

He sighed and slapped his hand on the counter. The two specimens leaped up and collided, landing together in a tangled mess. Dr. Cutter glared at them and dared them to do it again; they declined the honor. He swept the pile into his hand and was about to throw it into the trashcan when he impulsively stuck it under a microscope. Might as well take a look-see, he thought.

There in the bright light of the eyepiece, cells were in a frenzy of movement. The round-and-round genes had collided with the left-hand turn genes and were struggling for control. Finally, the cells started racing around in large circles. Counter-clockwise circles.

Large, strong, steady circles, on and on and on. Other cells stood on the sideline and watched.

Dr. Cutter clutched the counter with both hands to steady himself and watched the action. Thirty minutes later, he straightened up, rubbing his aching back and stiff neck; the cells were still at it. He didn't know what to make of it, but it excited him. He needed to take a headache pill, go lie down and explore the possibilities of what was happening in that sample.

Maybe he should ask Racer about it. Dr. Cutter hated to admit it. Even to himself that most of his great ideas had come from Racer. He walked around the room turning off equipment, putting things away and finally turned off the lights and headed back to his apartment on the company campus.

Night gave way to dawn and small sounds of day were heard in Plastic Genetics. No humans were there, as evil scientists tend not to be morning people. Mice, rats and hamsters were stirring, having their morning coffee, smoke, and water-cooler gossip.

Squeaker too, was enjoying a good stretch and scratch. Mornings were becoming a favorite time of day for her because she had developed a new skill. Unbeknownst to anyone, Squeaker had learned how to answer the phone and imitate Dr. Cutter's voice. Any vendor, salesman or outsider who called in the morning was apt to find himself the victim of a feline prank.

So far, she had doubled the order for cat tuna, bought three magazine subscriptions, told an I.R.S. investigator to go to Topeka, and given an interview to *Mad Scientist Monthly*. She pricked her ears; yes, that was a phone ringing down the hallway. Purring a jazzy tune, she sauntered towards the sound, wondering what poor sap was waiting for her today. She leaped up onto the desk, deftly hooked her paw under the receiver and flipped it off the hook.

"Yes, yes, Dr. Cutter here, who is it? Acme Body Parts? Do you have my shipment of human brains I ordered? Where are they from? D.C.! No, no, no! I specifically ordered mid-western brains. Everyone knows there aren't any brains worth a hill of beans in the D.C. area. Send them back! I can't waste my time on inferior stock."

Squeaker flipped the receiver back onto the cradle and grinned with self-satisfaction. What fun! Maybe she should learn how to use the computer; there was an opportunity to spread cat chaos! She made a mental note to make new friends in the administration office and spend time looking over their shoulders as they worked on their computers. Now to go back to her basket and look innocent as the staff started coming in.

Dr. Cutter hummed a little tune as he mixed and measured. Today he was going to try out this crazy left-hand-turn/round-and-round combination on some hamsters. He didn't think this accidental mix was of any importance; but last night his dreams wouldn't let go. Maybe if he played around with it, he could get it out of his system.

He measured out a portion and put it into the hamsters' favorite treat, whoopie pies. He diluted some of the mix and put it into another pie. Hamster A (Ralph) got the strong dose, and twenty other hamsters received the weaker mix. He then walked away, looking at his watch. I'll come back in an hour, he thought to see if there's any result.

With a sigh of annoyance, he headed downstairs towards the administration department. There was some nonsense about mixed-up orders, strange magazines and an irate phone message from an I.R.S. agent named Fleece that he wanted to discuss with the office manager, Mrs. Beiler. Couldn't anyone do anything right? And why did that name Fleece sound familiar?

Back in Lab 3C, Ralph was getting restless. He didn't mind working as a test animal, after all it was a job and jobs were thin on the ground these days, even for a rodent. Just don't call him a lab rat. Hamsters are a proud race and have always thought themselves better than mice and rats. Ask any rat and he'll give you an earful about what they think about hamsters.

Ralph twitched, scratched, got up and turned around. Another twitch, another turn. Then he felt the urge to run and run he did. Not on the exercise wheel like he usually would, but in a big circle on the cage floor. He didn't know why he was running; he just felt the need to be first; first at what, he couldn't say. It was as if someone was behind him and he had to stay ahead.

In the cage next door, the twenty hamsters that had received the weaker dose were also getting restless. Milling slowly around, not knowing what to do, they eventually noticed Ralph's mad race. One by one, they lined up against the cage wall and watched.

Watched and watched while Ralph ran and ran. Soon someone in the back of the crowd was cheering. "Come on, Ralph, you can do it!"

Ralph didn't know what they were talking about and neither did they, but somehow it felt right for everybody. Ralph enjoyed the attention he was getting and the other hamsters settled in for a good show. Someone called for pretzels and beer, but alas, there were none.

Dr. Cutter returned to his lab to check on his hamsters. There was Hamster A, running in a large counter-clockwise circle and there were the other hamsters lined up watching him.

Dr. Cutter couldn't say why, but he had this vague, uneasy feeling that they were…were….well, cheering Hamster A on. Dr. Cutter couldn't talk to these hamsters the way he could to Racer, so he couldn't ask them what was going on.

He set a timer and fixed a video camera on them and went to work on some other projects. He would ask Racer to talk to them and find out what was going on.

Racer didn't like to do this; he felt torn between his loyalties to Dr. Cutter and respect for the other hamsters' privacy. And then there was that little business about Hamster Union #316 which he hadn't told Dr. Cutter about yet.

Lefter entered the room and headed for the hamster cages. Checking the clipboards on each cage, he proceeded to give them fresh food and water, however, they ignored it. That was odd; usually they tucked right into it. Lefter looked a little closer. There was Ralph, still running in circles, although clearly he was tiring. And there was the crowd still watching him.

"What's going on guys?" asked Lefter, but it was as if he wasn't there.

Snap! Lefter felt a sharp rush of air near his right elbow. Snap! Snap! Lefter jumped back, it was Otto; he'd almost gotten Lefter. Otto was Dr. Cutter's Peruvian angelfire orchid. There was no need to feed Otto, he fed himself.

"Now, now" Lefter admonished him. "You know I'm off limits. Remember?"

Otto made no reply. He could speak, but seldom did. Sometimes he didn't speak for years and the staff forgot that he could. They also forgot that he could hear. Otto was a repository chock-full of scuttlebutt, office gossip and overheard telephone conversations. He was a better surveillance system than anything electronic.

Otto was permitted to eat the occasional wild mouse or rat that got into the building; but he was no longer allowed to eat any of the lab animals. Dr. Cutter had lowered the boom after Otto had eaten an especially

30

important rat that had been showing a gene therapy cure for male pattern baldness. Not that that a baldness cure had sufficient evil in it to appeal to Dr. Cutter, but it would have paid a lot of bills.

So, he had to take a firm line with Otto. "Now Otto, you can eat any wild rodent or insect that comes into the building, but you have to leave all the lab animals alone; and that includes Lefter," he said. But still, Otto couldn't resist taking an occasional swipe at somebody, just to see them jump.

Doreen sighed and looked down at the folder in her hand. Was she putting this into the filing cabinet or taking it out? She just couldn't concentrate on her work; Nelson was on her mind. She'd been a dedicated soldier in the war against the tobacco overlords and their evil empire for years now, unswayed by any distractions, but now Fate was taking her on a bit of a ride.

Fate, being bored one day, and having grabbed Nelson by the collar and thrown him into the ALA doorway, now proceeded to stir the pot by firing Cupid's darts at Doreen.

"Oh Mabel, don't you think he's dreamy?" sighed Doreen, as she twisted her hair around her finger. She drifted across the room waving the folder back and forth.

"Whoff ou u meanf ?" mumbled Mabel as she schnauzed in the candy jar for another root beer barrel.

31

Mabel had her priorities straight, she felt, and dreamy young men came far down the list after candy.

"What do you mean, who?" demanded Doreen. "Nelson, of course, that young man that came in here last week during that thunderstorm. Don't you think he's grand? He makes me think of a knight looking for a dragon, a hero looking for a challenge. I'm sure he's going to do great and noble deeds," she sighed and danced around the room with an imaginary partner.

"Oh, broffer!" snorted Mabel as she walked away. Such is the power of hormones to muck up one's view of a perfectly ordinary human being.

Nelson walked down the hallway, out the door and down the street. His third meeting of Nicotine Anonymous had just ended and he was not feeling very hopeful. Quitting smoking was a lot harder than he'd ever imagined.

He had tried cold-water plunges, standing on his head and even road apples; nothing helped. He was currently wearing three nicotine patches, chewing a stick of Nicorette gum, and smoking a cigarette.

Moodily, he made his way down the avenue and pondered his life. He had started out as a bright-eyed young lad, full of dreams and plans, eager to make his way as a writer in the big city. Subsequent experiences with profit-minded publishers and stonyhearted editors had turned him to the kinder, gentler world of the law; at least there, one could get a hearing.

Nelson wondered what turn his life would take next. Could he quit smoking and keep working for T.O.A.D.? Eventually someone would notice that he wasn't smoking anymore. Looks would be given, questions would be asked, and perhaps they would even make him take a drug test. The working world was a tricky place, all right. He threw his cigarette butt on the pavement and slid out the cigarette pack yet once again.

Government agent Percy Bumblebaum fidgeted, pulled down his cuffs and brushed off his coat sleeves. It was Saturday and poker night again. Percy was hoping for only two small miracles tonight, to win a hand against old Chesterfield and to forget about his job for a few hours.

He patted his pockets and felt for the comforting bulk of his package of antacids. The stress of working for the Bramble administration was taking its toll on him. Percy's job title was Process Administrator, a title so vague and boring that no one ever asked him what it meant. Which was a good thing, because he wasn't supposed to tell anyone what he really did. His job was to work in the background and raise money that the government could use without any public knowledge or accountability.

Lately funds were needed to continue the government's invasion of Quackii, which was ringing up the bills right and left. The Bramble administration had invaded Quackii because.....because.....well, the details were a little fuzzy, but Percy never bothered with details, not his department. What he really needed was a new idea, a new source of income. His office had worked the pet rock scheme and then the ugly baby-doll fad; but these didn't have any lasting power. He needed something long-term, something with staying power, something addictive. He sighed when he thought about T.O.A.D. and the hold they had on their customers. What a set-up!

Percy straightened and put on his game face as the door opened up. "Well, well boys, here we all are! Who's ready to lose money?" he asked. Dr. Cutter entered, followed by Burlington Chesterfield, two ethnic family crime organization heads, and seven international drug dealers in town for a convention.

Dr. Cutter replied "Not me, Percy boy. We bled you dry last time, I'm surprised you came back for more." Percy stiffened at the reminder and bit his tongue. He had a feeling he was going to need Dr. Cutter someday and he worked to keep on his good side.

"Well, maybe I'll get lucky this time, it's about time luck turned my way," he retorted.

Dr. Cutter snorted, "It's not luck that makes the man, Percy, its drive and intelligence, and more than a little evil. That's your problem, Bumble, you're just not evil enough. Give me a call sometime and maybe I can give you a few pointers. Now deal the cards and prepare to weep."

Dr. Linda stared aghast, at her friend and colleague, Dr. Helga. "Cut him open! What do you mean....cut open? How could you ...You...you wouldn't!" she finally blurted out. Panic ran riot in her head. "How could you think of doing such a thing? Lefter's our friend. And what would Dr. Cutter do to us, just answer me that?"

Unaccustomed tigress-defending-her-cub feelings were surging through her veins, she had to find a way to stop her friend's dangerous scheme. "And....and....and it's not like there's anything to see in there anyway. If he has any skinny-making qualities, it's going to be on the cellular level, you know that."

"I guess you're right," Dr. Helga replied regretfully. "It's just that I miss the old days, when you could open someone up and poke around and find out what was going on. Those old soothsayers with their gutted chickens knew what they were doing, I say. This new school of genetics lacks the grandeur and drama of surgery. Oh, Dr. Frankenstein," she intoned to the ceiling, "would that I had lived in your time!"

She looked sheepishly at her friend. She hadn't discussed much of her past with Dr. Linda; she sensed Dr. Linda lacked the proper amount of evil to appreciate those revelations.

Dr. Linda stood frozen, trying to juggle too many thoughts at one time. Did she have feelings for Lefter? How could she protect him? Was her friend capable of doing such a thing? And how do you get rid of a body? She shook herself fiercely. No, no, she had to come up with a way to divert her friend before something terrible happened.

"Look, Helga, we don't have to do it that way. I took a DNA sample from Lefter a while ago. Let's work with that and see if we can come up with something that will help us. We can use that new batch of hamsters that was bought at the farmers' market on Tuesday. I saw some plump Siberian ones in there that would be ideal test subjects."

"Oh all right, Linda. I didn't mean to upset you. I didn't realize you felt that way about Lefter. Let's go take a look at those hamsters before anyone else gets them." They walked together towards the shipping dock to check the incoming shipments. "And another thing, I want to see why there aren't any whoopie pies being sent to the lunchroom. Why should the hamsters get all of them?"

At the local Schwartz grocery store an experiment was in progress. T.O.A.D. lackey Kent Newport adjusted the video camera behind the one-way mirror in the deli department and turned it on. He was eager to see the results of the past year's collaboration with Plastic

Genetics. He rubbed his hands together in evil glee and sighed in satisfaction to be in on the beginning of another empire of slavery. Cows that produced nicotine and a sedative in their milk, only evil genius and greed could come up with such an idea. What a lucky boy he was, he thought.

The milk, made into cheese, was the product being tested today. Would the public buy it? Would they get hooked on it? And more importantly, would they continue to buy it, supposedly for its taste, not realizing they had been turned into nicotine addicts?

T.O.A.D.'s future might depend on it. If the American Lung Association drove the tobacco industry out of business, T.O.A.D. could easily switch over to nicotine cows and go on doing business that way. Of course, cheese would never have the panache and prestige of tobacco, but there you are; the world is a cruel place.

A family approached, the children whining and fighting over the cart and the parents doing the low-level bickering of the long-married couple. Kent moved out in front of the deli counter and took his position at the tray table. "Cheese, ma'am? Tasty and new, free samples today! Here, kiddies, a piece for each of you, and you, sir, give it a whirl. Put a little ketchup on it, just like at home. There you go, doesn't that hit the spot?"

The family munched and savored the bland, white squares they had been handed. Finished, they looked firmly at Kent. He knew what that meant, and he handed them more samples. Silence descended on the small group as the sedative took effect. Slowly, they smiled, straightened their posture and felt that perhaps the world wasn't such a bad place after all. They even went so far as to smile at their own family members.

The wife spoke up decisively, "We'll take two pounds, thank you."

Kent beamed at her, certain he was seeing history being made. It was the beginning of a whole new industry and he was in at the start. He beckoned another family to him, and built rosy castles in the air.

Dr. Cutter entered Lab 3C and walked over to Racer's cage. "How are you doing, old buddy? I haven't had much time to spend with you lately."

"I know, you've been working much too hard lately," Racer scolded. "You should get out more and get some fresh air. Maybe even do some exercise; I saw on TV that it's supposed to be good for humans. Makes them fit to live with, they say, but I don't know how you can tell with humans."

"You're right; maybe we could go out for a walk sometime. That would be good for both of us. Devil take it, let's do it now, the staff can keep an eye on things."

Racer's whiskers twitched with joy; he loved going outside. There was so much to see, and he could ask Dr. Cutter to explain anything, and he would. The public was so intimidated by Dr. Cutter they never dared ask him why he seemed to be talking to himself. Dr. Cutter slipped Racer into the pocket of his lab coat and went over to check his test hamsters.

Ralph was still lying where he had collapsed hours ago and the other hamsters were asleep in jumbled heaps. Replaying the tape he saw Ralph running and the others watching; then Ralph collapsed and a moan rose from the crowd. A few hamsters got out of their cage and went over to Ralph to try to revive him, with no success. The rest of the hamsters milled around, bumped into each other, quarreled and for lack of a better term, looked like they were drunk. Eventually they all settled down to sleep.

Dr. Cutter stopped the tape and tapped his finger on the counter. This mixture obviously had a powerful effect, but what use was it? Would it work on humans? Well, there was always one way to find out. He mixed up a new batch and walked downstairs to the loading dock.

"Let's see what this stuff can do, Racer. It's time for phase two of testing." Racer hung onto the pocket edge and took in all the noisy hustle and bustle around him. People hurried back and forth importantly, but somehow not much seemed to be getting done. Just like upstairs, Racer mused. Drivers hurried in and out of the break room, filling up on coffee and gossip. Dr. Cutter watched for a convenient test subject.

"Hey Dave, did you see all those trucks turned over down at the Buck? Pigs and molasses everywhere!" crowed Tom-Tom. "Bet you're glad you're not on the volunteer fire crew now! They'll be one good mess before this day's done."

Dave's face fell; actually, pigs and molasses did sound exciting, certainly more than the routine delivery job he had now. He sighed and walked over to the dispatch counter for his next assignment.

"What do you have for me, Patsy? For the love of sanity and civilization, don't send me down Route 30 again today; I've had as much of that as one person can take. If it keeps up, I'm going to have to get one of those bumper stickers. You know; the ones that say "I Drive Rte. 30 East, Pray for Me.""

"I can help with that," Patsy replied archly. "I have a boxful right here under the counter; for two dollars or a kiss, you can have one." She tilted her face up at him and smiled expectantly.

Dave turned red at this unexpected offer and fought down an urge to run. It wasn't that Patsy was unattractive, but she had this…this… faintly carnivorous aura about her. And no one knew whatever happened to her last boyfriend. He steeled himself, took a deep breath and prayed for an exit strategy.

"Uh…uh…uh" was all he managed to get out, as he kicked himself for not being able to come up with a better response. Get a grip on yourself, man, he scolded himself. She can't eat you. A sudden doubt chilled his spine and made his feet do a little jig of their own. His prayer's answer came just in time, with a welcome call from across the room.

"Hey Dave, look at this," someone called, waving a magazine. "The new tractor catalog's here! Wait'll you see this centerfold!" Dave slapped his coffee cup down with a splash and tried not to look like he was running away.

"Ur, ur, gotta see the boys about something," he stammered as he backed up and spun around.

Patsy sniffed and picked up her romance novel. The men in her books never acted like that. Maybe what men needed most was a good script writer, she thought. Her finger followed the dialog on the page and she soon lost herself in the latest adventures of Victoria Angela Maybelle Prime, real estate mogul of Manheim Township.

Dr. Cutter, seeing his chance, walked swiftly over and poured his mixture in the cup. Sliding away just as quickly, he settled himself in a corner to watch the results.

"Keep a sharp eye on him Racer," he whispered. "And watch the glory of genetics in action!"

Racer sat up in the breast pocket of the lab coat and took in the busy scene. "Which one?" he whispered back. "The one with green hair and three eyes?"

"No, no, that's one of Jones's experiments for Homeland Security that didn't work out. But we gave him a job down here working plain-clothes security. Blends right in, doesn't he? No, I mean the tall guy, over there in the plaid jacket. Let's see what happens when he gets a dose of that new mix."

Dave looked at the dispatch counter, saw that Patsy was buried in her book and took his chance to reclaim his coffee. He grabbed the cup, downed it in two gulps and went outside to light up a cigarette. He strolled back and forth, enjoying the fresh air and pondered his close escape.

Dr. Cutter followed him outside, anxious to keep him in view. Dave strolled back and forth, breathing deeply and stretching his arms. Soon he stopped, looking around in confusion. He twitched, scratched and turned around again. Turned left, he did. And turned left again. He stopped again, his muscles all bunched up, ready for he didn't know what.

Suddenly he burst into a full run down the driveway and out into the street. He hit the opposite sidewalk, narrowly missed a light post and a pretzel truck, and circled around back across the street to where he had started. Reaching the doorway, he made to go back inside but his feet had taken complete control and he swerved back across the street again. Arms flailing he made several large circles, drawing the attention of everybody in the area.

Across the street from Plastic Genetics was a Turkey Vulture Minit Market. In front of the minit market was what you find in front of every minit market in the c: loiterers, litterers and an unattended motor vehicle with its engine running. This one happened to be a hopped-up Chevy owned by one of the local young hoodlums. The young man had, for reasons known best to himself, no desire to chat with the police and had beefed up his car so as to avoid making their acquaintance.

Dave approached the car during one of his sweeps and it was only a moment's work to jump in, put it into gear and take off. Tearing out of the parking lot, he headed out for destinations unknown. Loud shouts sounded as he barely missed several pedestrians, a bakery truck, an Amish buggy and a police car. The police car turned to chase him. The car's owner came running out, commandeered a car and the chase was on.

Dave tore down the road, took the first left and put the pedal to the floor. A glance in the rear view mirror spurred him on. Had to stay in front, he told himself. He didn't know why, he just felt it in his bones.

He set his jaw and pushed his new car to its limits. People stopped in their daily tasks and watched the line of cars speeding down the road. Two more police cars joined the chase and several young men eager to be in on the excitement added to the confusion.

Dave saw another left and took it, his comet's tail of followers streaming out behind him. Up River Road, a narrow, twisty devil of a road, he sped into town. Past the town hall, the International Macaroni Museum, out of town and past the high brick walls of the madhouse.

Making large counter-clockwise circles around the town, he maneuvered his car back and forth so no one could get in front of him. Staying in front became his sole reason for being and he couldn't imagine doing anything else with his life.

The ruckus attracted more and more attention from the public. Drivers pulled over to get out of the way and people brought out chairs and sat along the curb to watch the action.

WPEQ, the local television station, called in their helicopter to cover the event and their van was already taping it for the six o'clock news. Street vendors popped up out of nowhere, using their ancient skills of smelling a sale. Hotdog vendors, soft pretzels, funnel cakes, whoopie pies, chicken corn soup and frozen sauerkraut on a stick; they were all there jostling for the best place. "Look once now, that's my foot you're standing on!"

Dr. Cutter stood on a small hill and watched the action unfold. Well, the mixture obviously had some kick to it, but how could he use it for evil? He scratched his chin and pondered his many customers, trying to find someone who would pay for this singular and bizarre behavior. Well, he'd have to sleep on it; maybe inspiration would come later.

Racer hung on the edge of the pocket and thoroughly enjoyed his outing. What a wonderful place the outside world was! There was so much going on, so many people doing their odd human things. He drank in every detail so he could tell it to his Wednesday night glee club.

The other hamsters never got out and they enjoyed Racer's stories, although they suspected he made much of it up. Everyone knew humans were unfathomable, but really; were they supposed to believe humans ran about on a grid, stopping and starting according to colored lights? Sounded like rats' work to them. The rat community had gotten wind of it and there was talk about unionizing and going on strike. Would humans go so low as to steal a rat's job? In these trying times, you could never be sure.

Dr. Cutter stood and watched the circle race until dark fell. With the coming chill, he decided to call it a day. "Come on, Racer, let's go home." He turned towards home, passing the minit market.

"Hrmph" Racer cleared his throat. "Uh…Dr., aren't you forgetting something?" He twisted back and forth anxiously looking at the store and Dr. Cutter's face. "It won't take a minute, you know. And besides, everyone knows that they're good for you, full of cholesterol and precious calories. Hmm mmm mmmm," he started humming. "You've seen that commercial on TV 'stop the world and have a whoopie pie'."

He waved his paws as he re-enacted the popular TV ad that all the hamsters in the lab loved. Not only because it featured their favorite snack, but also because it starred the vivacious and totally hot hamster actress, Smokey Velvet.

"All right, all right, my friend, we mustn't forget the important things in life. I wonder, Racer, if they would let me advertise my evil monsters on TV? They let T.O.A.D. advertise their cigarettes to the public, and that's a monster too, in a way. Why shouldn't I take advantage of TV too?"

"I don't think that's a good idea, Dr.; T.O.A.D. gets away with it because their ads show all those healthy, pretty young people running around looking like they're having the time of their lives. Very deceiving, that. I mean, how could you present your monsters in an attractive light?"

"Well, I could show monsters eating healthy, pretty young people….hmmm, no, I'm afraid you're right, it's a tough sell." He walked a couple of steps and stopped abruptly. "Video, that's the ticket! I could make videos and send them to select clients." He brightened up at the thought of increased sales and fame.

All aglow with his plans for the future, Dr. Cutter turned back into the store and came to a stop in front of the bakery section. Racer leaned far out from the pocket and checked out the selection of whoopie pies with an experienced nose.

"That one, third from the left. That's the one for us." He settled back in the coat pocket and enjoyed the busy scene of the minit market. Dr. Cutter reached out and picked up one and then another one. "We'd better get two, they're calling for snow tonight." They walked away slowly, munching in quiet satisfaction; even evil scientists like a little goodness.

Chapter 7

Nelson stood in the doorway and shuffled his feet as he worked up the nerve to approach Doreen. Steady boy, he told himself, deep breath and all that. It's like diving off the high platform, you only have to take the last step and do it.

While Nelson was lost in giving himself a pep talk, he noticed a movement by his side. Bringing his mind and eyes to focus, he found Doreen peering up at him.

"Are you all right, Nelson? Talking to yourself isn't a good sign. Come in and have some herbal tea." Nelson couldn't bring himself to tell her what he really thought about herbal tea, at least not this time. Let them be married for four or five years, he thought, then he might be able to tell her it was fit for nothing but cleaning out drains.

He lifted the cup to his lips without protest and soldiered on. "I've been trying everything," he told her, "but the tobacco devil has got a firm grip on me. How do other people do it? Can you help me? It has to be something on the quiet. If my boss at T.O.A.D. ever found out about, I'd be out on my ear in nothing flat."

"T…T…T.O.A.D.?" Doreen croaked. "You work for T.O.A.D.? I didn't know…. you mean you support their cause?" She stared at him while the rats of discord raced through her heart. Was her knight in shining armor a spy?

She clutched the counter behind her for support and tried to make the rats slow down and shut up so she could think. She knew T.O.A.D. was trying to infiltrate the ALA with spies; was Nelson one of them?

"You've heard of them? Of course you have, they're the biggest, richest company in the city," he said proudly. Doreen pointed wordlessly to the wall behind him. Nelson turned and saw a large poster of his boss, Burlington Chesterfield standing in front of the grand façade of the home office on Park Avenue. Across the top was:

> *T.O.A.D. Public Enemy #1*

and across the bottom:

> *America's biggest drug pusher*

"Oh…oh, I see. Yes, of course you know them. I…well; this is a bit of a mess, isn't it?

Doreen and Nelson looked at each other in dismay and neither of them knew what to say next. "I think you had better go now," Doreen choked out. "I can't think how you could do this to me. You're not the man I

48

thought you were. You'll have to find someone else to help you quit."

At these words Nelson went numb and the sun fell from his sky. "But...but...Doreen, it's not like that. I mean just because I work there doesn't mean I don't know that it's wrong. I only do it for the money. I'm beginning to think it shows, there's things going on there that they won't tell me about, something about cows. What in the world do they want with cows?" He stopped for a breath and saw that her heart had not been moved by his pleas for understanding. His heart sank even further as she silently pointed towards the door.

He rose and walked out, his mind in a whirl and his feet on automatic. Nelson had never given any thought to the conflict between his employer and Doreen's.

She really believes in what she's doing, he thought, I'm only at T.O.A.D. for the money. She'll never accept me as long as I work for them, but what can I do? A man has to work and T.O.A.D. pays good wages. He walked slowly back to Park Avenue and dully punched the elevator button for the fortieth floor.

Racer, Squeaker and Otto watched and listened as the lab staff reviewed last night's local news report.

"Did you see Dave on Channel 6 last night?" cried Dr. Linda. "What got into him? Why is it always the quiet ones that snap like that? WPEQ covered it live for hours, people couldn't seem to get enough of it."

"I know," Dr. Baker replied, "I stayed up late and watched the replays over and over. I even taped it so I can show the guys in my university class. I think I'll invite them over Saturday night and make a beer party out of it. That'll be a great time. I'm going to call Channel 6 too, and see if I can get a copy of all their footage. Everybody's talking about it!"

The talk continued in this fashion for some time. The lab animals had seen the coverage too, as the staff had forgotten to turn off the little TV in the lab. They had all watched avidly as Dave made local headlines.

"Humans are crazy," Squeaker declared, "no question about it. They have their uses, I admit, but they'll never reach the level of development that animals have. Running around in circles like that shows it."

Racer winced and growled to himself; that sounded like a hamster slur to him. But he steadied himself and struggled to make a civil reply. Sometimes he and Squeaker could put aside their dislike for each other and talk about ordinary, everyday things. He hoped they could reach a truce someday.

"I don't know," replied Racer, "studies have shown that humans have made great advances in their ability to live harmoniously with the world, and then they muck it up by having a war. You have to wonder if they'll ever get it right. But they seem to like to watch each other do things, maybe they could use that to calm themselves."

There was a small rustling sound and they both turned as Otto emitted a delicate belch and spat out a small bone. "Dave's round and round show sure packed in the crowd and kept them there for hours," he offered.

"Maybe if Dr. Cutter gave that mix to all humans, they'd be too busy watching to get into trouble. It sure would make life easier for the plants and animals in their world."

Squeaker and Racer looked at each other in surprise. That was the most they had heard from Otto in years. Once, Racer had asked, "Otto, what do plants do all day long?" and Otto had replied tersely, "Mind your own beeswax." After that, Racer left him alone, afraid to draw too much attention to himself.

It had never been proven that Otto had ever actually eaten a hamster, but Racer didn't want to take any chances. Mother hamsters used Otto to frighten disobedient youngsters into good behavior and horror stories were told about him late at night by the light of flickering test tubes.

Even Squeaker made sure to keep a safe distance from him. No one was really sure what Otto was capable of; one day he'd be on the windowsill of Lab 3C and the next day he'd be downstairs in the administration office. All the humans denied having moved him. Did he move himself? It was one of life's little mysteries.

Day drew to a close at Plastic Genetics and found Dr. Helga, Dr. Linda, and Lefter checking out the new shipment of hamsters. They made notes about which ones would be suitable for their experiment and in

51

return, thirty plump, sleek, sable-colored hamsters checked them out, making their own notes.

"We'll use all of these, half with the mix and half with a placebo," declared Dr. Helga. "Lefter, take them to my lab so no one else swipes them. Give them some whoopie pies so they get used to the taste of them. We're making history here, Linda. Think of it, no more diets, no more exercise; we'll be rich! We'll be famous! And best of all, we'll be thin! Who could ask for anything more?" She danced a circle around them.

Lefter gazed down at the new hamsters with a mixture of curiosity and regret. "Well, you guys are in for a ride. I don't think anything will come of this search for the fountain of thinness, but at least you'll eat good. That's one thing we know how to do in these parts."

"Thank you, sir. It's good to know we're in experienced hands, with someone who understands hamsters. We're pleased to be here." This speech came from Natasha, the largest female in the group. Lefter stepped back a step, startled by the unexpected words.

"Well, uh... uh... sure, sure" he stammered in reply. He was used to speech from hamsters that had been exposed to Three Mile Island's radioactivity for generations, but he hadn't known other hamsters might be able to talk. Well, he mused to himself, maybe I'll ask Racer and see if he knows anything about it. He picked up the cages and moved the animals to their new home and made them comfortable.

"I'll be back in a bit and see if you need anything," he told them. "I need to get on with my other work."

He walked away and busied himself with his daily routine of cleaning, feeding and errand running. Late afternoon found him in Lab 3C, cleaning Racer's cage. "We got new hamsters in, a nice looking bunch," he told Racer. He knew that Racer always enjoyed meeting the new hamsters and learning about where they had come from and what other hamsters did for a living.

"I'll go over this evening and talk to them," replied Racer. "But I also want to watch that footage of Dave again. Would you stay late tonight and play it for me?"

"Sure thing, I'd like to see it again, too. There's something about it that appeals to me. I can't figure out just what, though."

"Me too, it makes me shivery to watch him to go round and round. It makes me want to get on my wheel and run and run and yet at the same time it's more fun to watch him do the running."

Every so often Lefter would stay late in the lab and he and Racer would watch TV together and munch popcorn and drink beer.

Lefter knew Racer was smarter than he. But Racer never talked down to him and Lefter never treated Racer like he was a dumb animal; so they had developed a growing friendship.

"Okay, I'll be back around 7:00," said Lefter. "See you then."

Percy Bumblebaum nervously wiped his fingers before dialing the phone; he wasn't so sure that consulting Dr. Cutter was a good idea. If the newspapers caught wind of it, his career would be ruined. But he was desperate; pressure from above was growing, his boss had stepped up the demand for funds.

"Bombs don't fall out of the sky, Perry, we need more money," the big one would growl. Not only did Percy have to deal with the increasing demands, he was irritated that his boss couldn't even remember his name.

Percy was on the verge of correcting his boss, but something held him back. He had a vague feeling it might be better for him that the boss didn't know his name if the sauerkraut ever hit the fan.

He flexed his hands, took a deep breath and picked up the receiver. "Hello, Dr. Cutter?"

It was early morning (10:00 AM) when Squeaker heard the phone ring in Dr. Cutter's office. Without even stopping to wash and comb her whiskers, she raced down the hallway, looking forward to another opportunity to sow confusion and chaos in her part of the world.

"Hello, yes, yes, Dr. Cutter here. Who? Bumblebaum?" Squeaker dredged through her memory furiously, who was Bumblebaum? She didn't remember anyone mentioning that name in the lab. Oh, well, she'd play it by ear; after all, it was no tuna out her bowl if this Bumblebaum fellow couldn't make heads or tails of this phone call.

"What can I do for you, Bumblebaum? You need something to make money? Don't we all? I make monsters, not money trees, although that's not a bad idea. So what do want me to do for you?"

"Well," quavered Percy, "you know at the last game you said, 'Call me' so I'm calling. I need a long-running scheme, something addictive, something all-American. Something that will be so popular that no one will dare question it."

"You don't want much, do you, old boy?" replied Squeaker. She felt a little more confident now; she'd seen Dr. Cutter the day after a poker game and she felt certain that more than cards had been handed around. "I'll let you in on a new development, for a cut of 10%. It goes like this, see? I came up with this go-go juice. Makes some people run in circles for hours and weaker doses makes people want to watch it for hours. You could pass it off as a new sport or maybe a religion, something like that. Make up a fancy name for it and hire a PR company to sell it."

Squeaker started getting a little nervous. She'd never paid that much attention to humans and how they got things done, so she didn't know what else to tell him. She'd never really felt the need to study humans after she'd gotten Dr. Linda trained to take care of her. I'll have to start doing homework on humans if I want to keep this up, she thought. Note to self: spend more time in the Administrative office with Mrs. Beiler.

"Ur, I gotta go chum, one of my hamsters is on fire. Talk to you later, old boy." Squeaker hung up hurriedly. Well, that was enough for one day, time for a wash up and a nap. She wiped her paw prints off the phone and desk and headed back to her basket. Not that anyone would seriously suspect her, but better not take any chances.

Percy stared at the receiver in his hand and then slowly put it back in the cradle. Chum? Old boy? He didn't remember Dr. Cutter ever calling him that before. The Dr. didn't sound like himself today, but Percy couldn't quite say why. Well, what did it matter? The suggestion about go-go juice sounded wacky, but that's what Dr. Cutter was known for, off-the-wall ideas that actually worked.

He toyed with the idea of asking Dr. Cutter for a tour of his lab; he'd heard tantalizing rumors about that place. Better not, though. Better call his PR agency F.E.M.A. (Ferhoodled Enterprises Marketing Agency) and see how fast they could do a test market study on this stuff. He reached out his hand and dialed again.

Chapter 8

After Lefter decided to quit smoking, "WANTED" posters of the nicotine molecules were posted throughout his circulatory system. All systems were primed and ready for any invasion. White blood cells were mustered and given their marching orders: Nicotine, once our dear friend and treasured guest is now the enemy! He has turned out to be a foul deceiver, whose sweet promises were but poison dripped in our ear. He must be repelled at all costs; constant vigilance is the watchword! Barricades were set up around the lungs and lurkers were set up to watch the hands, so that they didn't light up a cigarette of their own doing.

Lefter watched as Dr. Linda peered into a microscope and clicked her tongue at what she saw, "I don't know what to make of it, Lefter. Some of the test rats are responding well to the gene therapy, but most show no improvement at all."

In the bright circle of light on the glass slide, Dr. Linda watched as Lefter's immune system cells battled with nicotine molecules. Lefter's cells spun rapidly, making the nicotine molecules feel dizzy and nauseous. The nicotine molecules were then easy prey for the white blood cells to slap cuffs on and bundle them off to the lock-up.

"I don't know what to say, Dr. Linda, maybe the rat has to want to quit to make it work. Rats can be powerful stubborn sometimes."

"Lefter, what an idea! Want to quit! Rats do what they're told, Lefter, nobody asked for their opinion on the tests we perform on them. They don't even have opinions, Lefter. They don't think like we do."

Lefter considered telling her about his years of experience in dealing with rodents, but decided now was not the time. Instead he took a deep breath, slipped his arm around her waist and planted a quick kiss on her lips.

"There," he said. "That's what I think. I've wanted to do that for a long time. What do you think of that?"

Dr. Linda blushed and stiffened while the rats of confusion and conflict ran riot in her head.

"Shut up!" she said to them. "How can I think with that racket going on? And what are you doing in my head anyway?"

"We are ghost rats, the spirits of all the rats that have died in all the experimental labs in the world. You were finished with us, but we aren't finished with you. This is our revenge, and we do so have opinions."

"Oh, is that all? Well, give me a break here. I think I'm falling in love with Lefter and I don't want to mess it up." She heard rat voices muttering in conference and then they were gone.

Dr. Linda smiled to herself and leaned warmly against Lefter for a long moment before straightening up and patting her hair.

"Not at work, Lefter. I don't know what your uncle would do if he saw us like this, but I don't think he'd like it." But she said it with a smile that told Lefter what he was so anxious to know.

"Will you see me tonight? I'll be here at the lab, no one will be here, and we'll have it all to ourselves. Say you'll come!"

Dr. Linda smiled. "Yes, I'll come. Now you should go, I don't want anybody else to know about us just yet."

Us! Lefter hugged the word to himself and repeated it over and over. Us! What a wonderful word! Lefter was walking on air as he went down the hallway but there was a question on the edge of his brain that wouldn't go away. Who was she talking to in her head?

Lefter hoped his new girlfriend wasn't being affected by the multitude of experiments going on in the building. Did she drink someone's test mixture by accident? There was that batch of Dr. Baker's that went missing last month; did someone put it into the coffeepot as a prank?

Lefter's head ached. He'd spent most of his life being careful not to ask questions and not to think; flabby mental muscles screamed with the unexpected effort. He headed to a janitor's closet he had set up for himself with a cot. He would just have a nice soft pretzel with plenty of mustard on it and then lie down for a while; that solved most problems, he found.

Nelson shuffled his papers, wiped the sweat from his brow and tried to calm his jumping stomach. The sun shone in the windows of T.O.A.D.'s main conference room highlighting the crags and valleys of the twenty faces turned his way.

It was time for Nelson to present his report on the legal aspects of the new advertising campaign, and he knew he'd made a hash of it. Between the nicotine withdrawal and his rejection by Doreen, he hadn't been able to concentrate at all. All he could see in his mind's eye was Doreen pointing to the door, her face ashen and withdrawn.

He tucked the wad of gum in his mouth into one cheek and tried to speak. "G..g..gentlemen, I have here an outline for each of you on our new campaign aimed at teenage gits, I mean girls. You'll see marketing research shows that teen girls are easily persuaded that smoking will make them more attractive, and medical research shows their brains are at the right age to develop a life-long addiction."

Nelson leaned across the broad table to hand outlines to the man across from him and he felt something slip. Just a little slip and a little clatter. He looked down to see what this distraction was and froze in horror. The contents of his shirt pocket had spilled out across the polished table for all the world to see. There were two pens, a bus transfer, a business card and a pack of gum; harmless enough at first glance. He reached out to gather it up before anyone noticed, but it was too late, Chesterfield had seen it.

"What's this?" he said, pouncing on the pack of gum. "Nicorette? You brought this tool of the devil into my company? I've always had my suspicions about you, Nelson. That quick energetic step, that pink, healthy complexion, they're not the hallmarks of the dedicated smoker we like to see here at T.O.A.D."

Chesterfield then picked up the business card and saw 'American Lung Association' in print on the front and scrawled across the back: Doreen 646-555-5555. His face, at first red, now began to climb through the color chart: tomato juice, beet juice, blood pudding and finally thundercloud black.

"Spy!" he roared, "a spy in our midst! A collaborator of the foulest sort! Seize him! Grab him, boys! Hold him down, I'll make him talk."

Nelson was vaguely aware he was hearing another voice. A small voice inside his head was trying to make itself heard over the commotion in the room. "Run!" it tried to scream, but it was only a whisper. "Blast, he's frozen up again. Bypass the frontal lobes and go right to cerebellum, engage feet and take us out of here." Nelson's inner survivalist took control, struggling through the sea of arms reaching out to restrain him and hustled him out the door.

Down the hallway, a quick right and then a left and he was at the back stairway. He clattered down the steps, leaping like a mountain goat.

After about five floors, his conscious mind woke up and said, "Hey, we're forty floors up. We can't do this all the way down. Take the elevator, stupid."

So he stepped out into a hallway, straightened his tie, smoothed his hair and tried to calm his racing heart. A quick elevator ride and he was on the ground floor and out the front door. He heard a kerfuffle behind him and turned to see the receptionist on the phone, gesturing wildly for him to come back. Not a chance, Nelson thought, and he quickly lost himself in the crowd.

Chapter 9

Dr. Cutter frowned at the phone and drummed his fingers on the desk. "Hello, Bumblebaum, what can I do for you? Go-go juice? What in the world are you talking about? The stuff I told you about last week?"

Dr. Cutter rummaged around in the junk drawer of his memory, looking for his last phone conversation with Percy, but he came up empty. *I don't remember ever talking on the phone with him, I only ever see him at the monthly poker game,* he thought.

Well, he'd been working hard lately, putting in long hours trying to make a flying pig, so maybe he had tossed that memory out completely. "Refresh my memory, Percy. I've been working overtime lately. Uh-hum, Uh-hum, oh, that stuff. You really want to give that a try? All right, I'll send some over with instructions about dosage. Your firm can work on it from there and see if anything works out for you."

Dr. Cutter hung up the phone and once again tried to summon up last week's conversation about the go-go juice. Nope, not a crumb of it could be found.

He was starting to get worried about himself. There seemed to be more and more things happening that he didn't remember doing. Like telling off that I.R.S. investigator; that scared him. He couldn't remember doing that, it wasn't like him at all. Normally he tried to keep a very low profile. Was he getting senile? How would he know? He didn't have anyone he could trust.

Well, I'll think about it later, he decided. He put those thoughts on a shelf and shoved them out of sight. Then he went to his lab, mixed up a fresh batch of go-go juice and sent Dave to take it to Bumblebaum's office.

The sun was sinking low over York County and reflecting golden rays off the Susquehanna River as quiet settled over the Plastic Genetics campus. Lab technicians turned off equipment, slammed their locker doors shut, and shouted good nights down the hallway. Footsteps faded away and Lefter was finally alone; the day had seemed like it would never end. He hurried upstairs to the third floor lounge and put down his packages.

Beer, hard pretzels, chips and red beet eggs were unpacked on the side table. A quick check of the fridge showed the necessities of life – catsup, mustard, pickles and soda pop – were on hand.

He debated over lighting a candle. It would set the mood; but better not. If something caught fire, there'd be no end of trouble. He took a last look around and walked across the hallway into Lab 3C and over to Racer's cage.

"Are you ready, Racer?" he asked. "I asked Dr. Linda to come and watch too. I hope she likes it as much as we do."

He hesitated, trying to remember if he had actually said anything to Dr. Linda about watching TV tonight. A quick check of his memory banks came up with a warm, fuzzy pink glow, but no speech records. What had really happened this afternoon?

Racer stretched up and climbed onto Lefter's hand. "I hope so too, but you can never tell with females," he replied. "Things that make perfect sense to males seem to mystify them. I tried to explain a tractor pull to a group of females the other day and they just giggled. You see, it all started out when one farmer said to another farmer, 'My tractor's bigger than your tractor,' and the other one said….."

"We got a new batch of hamsters in yesterday, Racer," Lefter reminded him. "I know you'll want to go over and see them. One of them can talk! I didn't know other hamsters could do that It's not common is it?"

"It doesn't happen too often, Lefter. Usually it takes generations of living near nuclear waste to do it. I'll go over later on tonight and visit with them and see where they're from. I wonder if they know the Oyster Creek clan?"

They went to the lounge and settled in to warm up the tube. Lefter put out a pretzel and poured some hard cider for Racer. He leaned back on the couch and ran his finger repeatedly around his collar and tried to look relaxed.

"Say, Racer, do you know anything about females?" he stammered nervously. "I mean, you know, wh... wh... what they're thinking, and how... how... how do you know if they really like you?" Lefter gulped and blushed as he looked hopefully at his friend.

Racer reluctantly tore his eyes off of the TV and turned his attention to his anxious friend.

"Well, with hamsters, it's pretty straight-forward. If the female doesn't run away from you and doesn't try to tear your throat out you've got a good chance. And there's always the smells they put out too, that's a big help. But you humans seem to have lost your sense of smell, so I don't know how humans signal each other. I think Dr. Linda really likes you. She smiles real warm at you and it makes Dr. Baker grind his teeth. Females like to think they're in control, so relax and let her take the lead. It'll come out right in the end."

Soon hurried footsteps were heard in the hallway and Dr. Linda rushed through the doorway. "Ohhhhh Lefter, who is that horrible man at the front door? He demanded to see Dr. Cutter and I told him the lab is closed and he said he knows what goes on in here and he tried to push past me and... and... and... ohhh, he was frightening."

Lefter jumped up and hugged her tightly. "I didn't see anybody when I came in. I'll go downstairs and look around. You stay here with Racer; turn loose the guard monsters if you hear anybody break in. You know he doesn't want the police here."

He looked around for something dull and blunt and spotted some stale fasnachts on top of the fridge. He grabbed two handfuls and ran out the door. Dr. Linda and Racer looked at each other, worry wrinkles on both their faces.

Fasnachts are made for Fat Tuesday every February, and for the following two weeks, assault rates in Lancaster County are sure to rise. A stale fasnacht soon hardens into a legally classified blunt instrument. Lancaster's district attorney routinely tries to haul in the church and firehouse volunteers who make them; but the charge of supplying ammo to thugs never sticks.

"Racer, do you know who that man is?" Dr. Linda asked, twisting her hands over and over.

"No, I don't remember Dr. Cutter saying anything about expecting company. You know he discourages outsiders coming around the lab. The mayor and the city council wanted a tour when this place was built and he gave them the cold shoulder; he told them it wasn't safe. I'm not sure that was a good idea, politicians can be awful touchy," he replied.

As they gazed at each other, a shadow slipped through the doorway and under the sofa. Squeaker Cat had heard noises in the lounge and she didn't like to miss out on any action. Anything from a dropped morsel, a bald-faced lie, a whispered confidence or an outright quarrel, she liked it all. She settled herself in a dark corner and waited to see what would happen next.

Lefter came up the stairs, a golf club in his hand and a satisfied look on his face. "I don't know who he was, but he's hurting now. I got him good with three fasnachts right in the head. Those ones from Weavers, you know, they make them like boat anchors. He won't be sneaking around here anymore."

Bit by bit they calmed down and after talking a little about the stranger, they forgot him and turned their attention to the TV. Lefter put the tape in and they watched Dave go round and round on the screen.

"Look at him go!" cried Lefter. "He's a genius with that car, no one can beat him! Look at that red car trying to get in front of him. He keeps cutting him off....ohhh, right into the river! He'll be lucky if the rescue squad gets him before the snapping turtles do."

"Go Dave, go!" cheered Racer. He was sitting bolt upright, his whiskers twitching wildly, his eyes never leaving the screen. "I'd like to be in the car with him and see all those other cars eat my dust! What a ride!"

Dr. Linda watched the screen for a bit, but soon found it was more interesting to watch Lefter and Racer. She was interested in the race, but not as avidly as the other two were. Maybe it's a male thing, she thought, competition and all that. She sniffed in self-satisfaction. Women never competed with each other like that; they just liked to look nice, is all. And if they wanted to look nicer than everybody else, well, they were only doing their best, that's all.

They watched the tape three times before they had enough and turned to the evening news. Dr. Linda turned the lights down low and snuggled up against Lefter. He slipped his arm around her and they were soon lost to the world.

Racer saw a good opportunity to slip out and he was soon in the hallway, headed towards the lab that held the new hamsters. Racer was an outgoing hamster and liked to meet new friends and help them get settled in what he considered his building.

He licked a stray pretzel crumb off of his whiskers and sang a hamster folk tune as he headed out, "Now is the time for all good hamsters to dum-de-dum-dum…" He didn't travel alone; Squeaker squashed herself flat into a pool of shadow and watched him go down the hallway.

A quick scramble up a lamp cord and Racer was on the counter top looking at the new hamsters. "Hi there, my name's Racer. Welcome to Plastic Genetics. Where are you from? Tell me everything. I love to hear about other parts of the world."

The group of new hamsters huddled together and stared at him silently.

Now what? Racer thought. Don't tell me they can't even understand hamster talk. Why don't they say something? He had never seen such large hamsters in his life; he shuffled his feet nervously and puffed up his fur to look as big as possible.

A large, dark female pushed her way to the front of the group and looked Racer up and down. She seemed to be the leader of the group. She had an 'I'm-the-boss-around-here' air to her.

"Thank you, sir, my name is Natasha and we're looking forward to working here. Even in my homeland we've heard of Dr. Cutter and his marvelous monstrous creations."

She continued talking, but Racer didn't take in much of it in. He was smitten by this zaftig vision of loveliness in front of him. She was large, plump, sleek and dark-eyed, all the features that hamsters find attractive in each other. Hamsters have no understanding of humans' quest for slimness.

He continued to stare at her moon-eyed while she talked. He dimly gathered that her clan was originally from Siberia, but her branch was from a mysterious land to the east called Joisey, and she had the exotic accent to prove it.

The visit continued while the moon rose high and began to set. Finally, Racer said goodnight and headed back to his cage. As he moved along the counter he caught a rushing shadow out of the corner of his eye. Squeaker had seen her chance and leapt forward to snatch him up. She knew she didn't dare kill him but she couldn't resist the opportunity to smack him around a little, at least until she felt better.

One leap gained her the chair, another took her to the counter top and then she roared down on Racer like a vacuum cleaner, every hamster's terror. Racer lost no time in wheeling around and kicking into high gear.

Down the length of the counter, he jumped from machine to machine and finally reached a windowsill. The window was open a few inches and Racer didn't even have to crouch to get under it. All those hours on the exercise wheel stood him in good stead as he scrambled down the ivy-covered wall and across the lawn.

Tossing out a quick plea to St. Hambright the Bold, the patron saint of hamsters in mortal peril, he sped into the darkness and safety. Back in the building, Squeaker howled in frustration as she scratched vainly at the window, trying to get out.

Chapter 10

Percy Bumblebaum stood on the top row of seats and felt a growing satisfaction at the size of the crowd below. The Zoomer Juice race trials were growing larger and larger with every event and promised to get bigger yet.

"It's a gold mine!" he shouted to no one in particular. Percy danced a little jig and patted himself on the back for being such a fine fellow. Life was good for a change.

Percy had seen the TV footage of Dave's race with the police and recognized him when he arrived at his office to deliver the mixture. He listened intently as Dave told him of his exhilaration of outrunning the police until his car ran out of gas.

"It was wild, man!" screamed Dave, waving his arms in emphasis. "It's the greatest thing I've ever done. I wanted to bury that cop car in my dust, and that was my brother back there! I don't know what's come over me, but now I want to race everything in sight. People keep challenging me on the streets and it's hard to resist. What am I going to do, man?" he asked Percy in desperation. "I can't keep getting arrested for speeding, or Mom will come up from New Texas and take my car keys away." He shuddered at the thought and looked down and clutched his keys tightly.

Percy gazed at the excited young man gesturing in front of him and sensed an opportunity. He reflected on the extensive TV coverage of the events, and his head whirled with jumbled images. His mind saw flashing police lights, screaming car engines, and rapt faces watching the action and cheering. Enthusiasm equals money, he reminded himself, so how can I tap into this?

"Hmm, hmm, hmm," he wuffled through his thick mustache, not having a ready answer to give to Dave. He knew there was an answer somewhere; he just couldn't see it at the moment. He looked down at his empty hand, surprised and annoyed that the answer wasn't there.

"Let me work on a couple of ideas and get back to you," he finally replied. "I know there's something we can do with it. I just don't know what yet. Here, take my business card. Don't lose it, I'll be in touch."

Percy handed him a business card, a hefty tip and gave him a hearty slap on the shoulder. He turned back to his desk, every mental cog and gear whirling at high speed. He could smell money, he could almost touch it, and his hunting instincts sat up and sniffed the wind. Percy, the mighty money hunter was on the prowl again. He growled to himself as he pulled the phone closer to him and started to dial.

The answer was racing, Percy found out after a hard day of scratching diagrams on his think pad. Racing with the extra edge that go-go juice would provide.

He pondered the idea of introducing a religious theme to the business. Nope, probably wasn't necessary, he decided. Besides, priests had a way of getting underfoot and becoming hard to handle. He drew a line through that notation.

He looked at his financial diagram and nodded his head in approval. Extracting money from the public without causing a fuss was a delicate task and required the sure hand of a professional, and Percy knew he was the right man for the job.

"Percy, my boy, you've done it again," he assured himself smugly.

With Dave's enthusiasm fresh in his mind, Percy offered Dave the spot as Zoomer's first racecar driver. Dave looked dazzling in his silver jumpsuit and he strutted up and down beside his shiny new car painted with the lurid Zoomer Juice logo.

"What about it, boys?" he taunted the crowd of young men looking at him enviously. "Think you can beat me? Put your money where your mouth is, and show me!"

He sneered at them and instantly made enemies. Dozens of young male hearts hardened against him and vowed his doom. Their sisters simpered and pranced and a different sort of competition bloomed in their hearts. Dave didn't know it but his life was about to get much more complicated.

Small groups of racing fanatics quickly formed teams and pooled their skills to beat the smirk off of Dave's face and win cash and bragging rights. Hundreds of their friends and family showed up at every race to cheer them on and place their bets.

Ferhoodled Enterprises went whole-hog promoting the new pastime. Posters were everywhere, screaming 'Go! Go! Go! Go to the Races!' Radio and TV ads stridently informed every person on the east coast that there was something new bubbling up in Lancaster County. 'Zoomer Races are starting now. Everyone's here, so where are you?' they goaded people shamelessly.

The unsubtle threat of being left out of something new drew customers in by the thousands. They came, they saw, they ate it up with a roaring appetite. Fan clubs popped up overnight and friendly rivalries were formed. "Yah, yah! My grandmother can drive better than your driver. Tell him to go back to his buggy." "Yeah? Come over here and say that!"

On opening day balloons and streamers were everywhere, a live band played near the front gate and a large banner hung across the entrance to the racetrack. Just inside the gate were booths handing out free samples of Zoomer Juice in assorted flavors (beer, cola, tobacco chaw, pineapple) to every man, woman and child who passed them. Dr. Cutter had recommended doses of 1ml for adults, but F.E.M.A. had muddled it and instead mixed up 100ml doses and handed out free samples to everyone they could find.

The result wasn't people who were mildly interested in racing, but people who were rabid fans. They became people who would spend every free moment and every available dollar to follow their favorite driver or team. Business was brisk and Percy Bumblebaum was a very happy man.

Next to the Zoomer Juice booths T.O.A.D. set up a booth to hand out hotdogs wrapped in slices of Nikki Cheese, Nikki cheese-covered onion rings and deep fried Nikki cheese chunks. They too, were doing a brisk trade. Further along the path the purveyors of chicken corn soup; red beet eggs, cup cheese, and soft pretzels were glowering in their direction. How was a body to do business with that kind of competition going on?

WPEQ covered the races from the beginning and their audience grew beyond their wildest dreams. Many sponsors rushed in to take part in the feeding frenzy. Every company selling shoes to toothpaste to Mrs. Stoltzfus's Shoo-fly Pie had ads plastered on every available surface. Even the racecars had not escaped their advertising frenzy. Zook's Miracle Oil and Mrs. Hess's Brown Eggs were prominently displayed on most of the car doors. T.O.A.D. was touting their cigarettes at this venue, and introduced their new product, Nikki Cheese (Modern Cheese for the Modern Family).

Dr. Cutter glared across the desk at the red-faced man glaring back at him. It was late evening and Dr. Cutter was in the administration office trying to complete his expense account while waiting for his eight o'clock appointment with an I.R.S. investigator. And here he was, Fleece, of all people – he hadn't seen that one coming.

"So Fleece, what do you want with me? And what happened to your face? I heard you went to work for the I.R.S. Is that from one of your fans?"

Large purple bruises covered Fleece's face and a black eye completed the ensemble. He reached up and gingerly touched the swellings. "I was here last night to see you and that idiot nephew of yours threw rocks at me! Rocks covered with powdered sugar. What's that all about; some quaint local custom? But that's not what I'm here for. I want money and you're going to give it to me!"

"Money! Fat chance! Why would I want to give you money? As if you don't skim enough off everybody you meet. Get lost and stop wasting my time."

"Not so fast, Cutter. I know what goes on in here; I have my sources. You pay me nicely and I'll keep my mouth shut. If you don't, I'll spill the beans about that Zoomer Juice you created. Gene therapy en masse to addict people to squeeze money out of them! Just wait until the press gets hold of that! They'll have a field day with it, and the locals will burn this place down. I've been waiting to get you ever since you put that stink bomb in my locker."

Dr. Cutter felt ice rats running up and down his spine as he tried to make sense of it all. Percy worked for the government and so did the I.R.S., so why was Fleece here? Jealousy? Greed? Interdepartmental competition? Or was it just another example of one government hand not knowing what the other hand was doing? What did it matter? The question was what to do this minute.

As he paced up and down the room, stalling for time, he tried to remember his schooldays at Evil University. Fleece had been a couple of years ahead of him and even then had a reputation as a weasel. He'd been voted as the one most likely to do well in government, one of the school's highest honors.

Planting stink bomb surprises had been a popular pastime of Cutter's youth, although he couldn't remember everyone he had targeted. But enough of fond reminisces, what was he going to do about this threat before him? Maybe if he gave him some cash now, he could hold him off for a while until he could think of a better solution.

"All right, all right, don't get your feathers all ruffled. I have some money upstairs in my office. You wait right here and I'll bring it down." He headed out the door, thinking, so Lefter does have some uses after all. Pity he didn't throw Fleece in the river and let the giant catfish eat him. He knew he didn't have any money in his office and he went up the stairs slowly, trying to think of a plan.

Back in the administration office, Squeaker looked down at the pacing form of Fleece from the top of a tall filing cabinet. She'd heard the entire conversation and anger and fear poured through her veins. She didn't give a rat's tail about Dr. Cutter but she knew which side her tuna was buttered on. If the lab closed down then Dr.

Linda would be out of a job and she wouldn't be able to support Squeaker anymore; besides, she liked Dr. Linda.

She lashed her tail and gathered her feet under her, ready to jump. She'd never tried to bring down anything as large as a human before, but she knew she had to do something. It was obvious to her that Dr. Cutter didn't know what to do, so it was up to her.

"Hey Fleece!" she called to him in Dr. Cutter's voice. With a silent prayer to any gods that might be in the neighborhood, she launched herself into the air.

Fleece heard his name and looked up in time to get a face full of desperate cat. Squeaker scratched and bit for all she was worth and Fleece stumbled about, cursing and flailing his arms.

"Aghh…Get off me! Help! Help!" he appealed to the empty room. His mind raced wildly with all the outrageous stories his informant had given him, about monsters and freaks of nature living here. His hands scrambled wildly for something to hit with.

"Die, you mangy skunk! This is my turf, you can't have it," Squeaker roared, with as deep a voice as a nine-pound cat can muster. She dug in with every ounce of strength she had and tried to claw a hole through the front of his shirt and out the back.

Back and forth across the room the two carried out their dance of death until Fleece's heel caught the braided rug in front of the door and he fell backward against the window.

"Hold still," Squeaker cursed. She tried to work her way around to the back of his neck to deliver the killing bite on his spine when she heard a great whooshing, rustling sound. Otto was sitting on that particular windowsill and he too, had witnessed the threat to his home. Although Otto had wild ancestors, he was a houseplant and he *liked* being a houseplant. He had no intentions of being thrown into the wild to fight it out with all the nasties out there.

Otto expanded himself like a rubber band and tightly wrapped his tendrils around the toppling man. Squeaker jumped off in the nick of time and fled under the desk. Gasping raggedly she whirled around and watched the strange scene unfolding. Although Otto was known as an orchid, his grandmother (on his mother's side) had been a strangler fig and he now drew on this ancestry to take care of business. He knew that genetics, intelligently used, could evolve into some very useful designs.

A quick, strong squeeze broke the spine of the agent, and then Otto proceeded to compact Fleece into a handy bite-size morsel. Chomp, chomp, chomp and the deed was done. Otto belched and stretched and settled himself back into a small, harmless looking form. The only thing left was a business card that he spat out.

Squeaker watched as the card silently floated down to the floor in front of her. She didn't know which god to thank for this turn of events, so she just said thank you. She tried to calm her jangling nerves by doing a quick lick and brush up, and paused at the sound of footsteps in the hallway.

Dr. Cutter returned to the office carrying a bottle of whisky liberally laced with a box of rat poison he'd found in the janitor's closet and some ground up sleeping pills he had in his desk. He didn't know if Fleece would be foolish enough to drink it, but it was all he could think of.

He looked around and called, "Fleece, where are you? Let's have a drink and talk about this. I'm sure we can work something out."

Silence met him and patted him on the shoulder. It was a peculiar silence, one that had the quiet air of a great event just finished, with echoes of glory and cheering still faintly heard on the wind.

Dr. Cutter looked around; spotted the business card on the floor and picked it up. He called again, and checked the back office and the bathroom: nothing. He scanned the front office again

There was that cat again, hiding under the desk, the rug askew, the curtain torn halfway down. It didn't add up. What would cause the cat to tear the place up and make Fleece leave?

His gaze fell on Otto and he walked over to see if he'd been damaged. He looked bigger than he had this morning, more... sated somehow. Then his eye caught a few threads on Otto's leaves, and he noticed the particular glow that meant Otto had just had a good feed.

"You didn't!" he gasped. "I mean... you couldn't... not something that big. Could you? Oh gods, what am I going to do now?" A darker thought came to him suddenly. "Racer, what about Racer? You didn't eat him too?"

Dr. Cutter noticed earlier in the day that Racer was missing from his cage and he was worried sick about it. Seldom did Racer go away without telling Dr. Cutter where he was going. He searched the building and grilled the staff with no success. And now on top of this worry, he had a missing government employee to explain away.

"Nope, not Racer. Haven't seen him since last week," said Otto. "Didn't think you'd mind about the tax man. I mean, he's not in the off limit group. Besides, there's plenty more where he came from." He said it in a smiley kind of voice that gave Dr. Cutter the shudders, and he wasn't a man to shudder easily.

"Still… still… you can't go around eating people. I mean, what will I tell people? They'll come looking for him, won't they?" Dr. Cutter pleaded with him.

"I can too go around eating people; I just did. And they won't come looking for him. He wasn't here on official business, he was… what do you call it? Dark mailing you. Can't have that sort of thing around here," he sniffed, "it lowers the morale."

Dr. Cutter looked at the bottle in his hand and mindlessly brought it up to his lips for a deep swig. He had never felt a stronger need for a drink than right now. Just in time he remembered the poison and put the bottle down.

"I think I need to go home now and have a nice lie down; maybe with a bottle, maybe with two bottles. What a day, what next?" He tottered to the door and let himself out. Wearily he headed towards his apartment and for the first time in his life, he thought about retirement.

Chapter 11

Fate grabbed Nelson as he hurried away from his dead career at T.O.A.D., hustled him into the train station and onto a waiting train he had deliberately stalled for this purpose. Now that his cargo was aboard he started the train up, and let the other commuters get on with their lives.

Nelson sat in a daze, eventually waking up to the soothing green countryside rushing by his window. He wondered vaguely why he'd gotten on the train. The train stopped and Nelson exited the train without any idea where he was, where he was going, or why he should get out at this stop. Walking out of the station he chose a street that took him away from the center of town.

Up one street and down another Nelson walked for hours, trying to figure out what to do with himself. His job at T.O.A.D. was a goner, his relationship with Doreen over, and he didn't know what to do next. Stopping at a corner he leaned up against the building and pulled out his pack of cigarettes. Just as he had finished lighting up, he heard a voice. "Um… hey mister."

Nelson jerked himself upright and looked around. The voice sounded like it was coming from behind him and how could that be when he was leaning up against a wall? Also, the voice sounded small, sort of… rodenty like. He scanned the area swiftly, ready to take off. He had been hearing voices lately, and with all the things that had happened to him this week his nerves were more than a little unstrung.

"Here I am, right in front of you," said the voice again. "Down on the windowsill." Nelson leaned in and looked a little closer. Indeed, there was someone, rather, something there. A closer inspection revealed a golden brown hamster on the windowsill.

"Hiya, how ya doing? My name is Racer. Could you do me a favor?"

Nelson groaned and rubbed his eyes. As if hearing voices wasn't enough, now he was hallucinating too. A talking hamster, what next? He felt a deep longing for his old therapist Dr. Tell-Me-Everything and his cozy, familiar office. Dr. Tell-Me-Everything would be able to explain this away, he always could. 'Too much work, Nelson, not enough exercise, Nelson,' he would say. 'And take these little blue pills, they work on everything.' Nelson felt his pockets in vain; he had long ago used up his bottle of blue pills and hadn't gotten around to refilling it. Even as he searched his pockets he knew that even the little blue pills would be out of their league here.

"Er... Hi... Er... what do you want?" Great, Nelson thought, now I'm talking back to my hallucination, that's not a good sign. Still, no matter how much he rubbed his eyes, that hamster wouldn't go away. He was still there, sitting up on his hind legs and peering at him near-sightedly; much like his dotty Aunt Petunia.

"I need to get back home," Racer went on. "I was chased by a cat and lost my way. I've been here for days and I'm starving. Could you take me to the Plastic Genetics building, please? I'll see that you're well rewarded for your trouble."

Nelson hesitated and started backing away. "Uh, sorry, not going that way, uh... have an appointment, uh... uh... sorry." Nelson didn't know why he was apologizing to a hallucination, but it seemed right.

"Pleeese? I know this looks strange," pleaded Racer, "but I really don't know what else to do. A gang of rats nearly got me in that alley back there, and I think they're still watching. Oh gods, there's a cat behind you!"

Nelson jerked around and saw a stringy gray tabby measuring the jump from street to windowsill with a knowing air. Meanwhile, Racer sent a prayer to St. Hambright to move this man's heart.

"Oh gods, don't let the cat get me," Racer moaned.

Fate firmly prodded Nelson between the shoulder blades and Nelson slowly started moving. He pushed the cat aside with his foot and numbly picked up Racer and walked in a daze down the street.

"I think we should head towards the river," Racer said breathlessly. "It's between the town and the river, I know that much."

Great, thought Nelson, then I can throw myself in the river and get all this over with. Stopping a passerby, Nelson received directions to Plastic Genetics, found the building and headed up the walk to the back door. Before he could ring the bell, the door opened and Dr. Linda came out.

"Yes, can I help you? We don't see salesmen without an appointment, you know."

Nelson wordlessly held up Racer and gave him to Dr. Linda.

"Racer!" she cried. "Racer, where have you been? We've been looking all over for you, and Dr. Cutter hasn't been able to think of anything else but you."

Nelson gaped. He tried not to, he'd been brought up better than that, but it had been a long day and he was having trouble taking it all in.

"You talk to him?" he queried Dr. Linda. "Does he... you know ... talk back? I mean do you hear him talk? I'm sorry, I don't mean to be rude, but hamsters can't talk... can they?"

Dr. Linda smiled and took his arm. "I understand, it was a shock to me too, at first. But you get used to it, and really, he is a great conversationalist. Come in and have a cup of coffee."

"Dr. Linda, I promised this nice man a reward for helping me," said Racer. "Please see that he's taken care of."

"Of course we will, Racer. We're so thrilled to have you back. Come in, Mr...? I'm sorry, what is your name?"

"Hambright, Nelson Hambright. Call me Nelson, or call me crazy, it doesn't much matter anymore," he replied. "I don't know which side is up anymore. Do you have anything hard to drink?"

Dr. Linda led Nelson into the lounge, sat him down in an easy chair and put Racer on the side table. She then busied herself making a pot of coffee and called upstairs to Dr. Helga.

"Helga, tell Dr. Cutter that Racer's back! And come down to the first floor lounge, we have company," she said joyfully.

Dr. Linda felt a dark weight lifting off her shoulders. Now that Racer was back, she felt everything would go back to being normal.

Racer's absence had cast a pall over the entire building. Workers had shifted nervously throughout their day, huddling in groups, exchanging the most recent rumors. Some said Racer had been kidnapped by a rival science lab and was being held for ransom. Some said he had been nabbed by government agents, and held until Dr. Cutter had performed some dark task.

That last rumor didn't make any sense since most of Plastic Genetics' output was dark tasks. All everyone knew was with Racer gone, Dr. Cutter wasn't happy and when Dr. Cutter wasn't happy, thunderclouds rumbled all throughout the building.

Nelson pulled out his pack of cigarettes and fumbled to get one out. To his horror he realized the pack was empty.

"Oh great, that's just great! I never needed a cigarette more than I do now and the pack's empty." He threw the empty pack on the table and slumped down in the chair and buried his face in his hands. "A thousand curses on T.O.A.D. and all their kind. I feel like I'll never be free of them, they'll follow me to my grave. No, actually, they'll dig my grave for me, one cigarette at a time. You never saw such evil as that crowd. You have no idea the kinds of things people those people will do for money."

Dr. Linda and Dr. Helga looked at Nelson and then at each other. Silently they agreed this was not the time to explain to Nelson exactly where he was. It looked as if he had enough to deal with for one day.

Dr. Helga heated up some chicken pot-pie and set out celery, butter bread and red beet eggs. She knew all about the powers of addiction and knew Nelson was going to need all the help he could get to throw it off.

"I know how it feels," she said. "I thought I could never quit smoking, but I did it. Dr. Linda here has been working on a nicotine vaccine precisely for people like you. Pity it's not ready for human trials yet."

Nelson leaped from his chair and threw himself on his knees in front of Dr. Linda. "Let me try it, I'm begging you. My life can't get any worse than it is now. My life has been a nightmare this past week and I'm not sure I'm sane anymore."

He glanced sideways at Racer who was working on a hard pretzel and oblivious to everyone, and then shuddered and tore his gaze away. It was too much to ask a man to believe, he felt.

Nelson poured out his whole story to his rapt audience. He proceeded to tell them all about his working for T.O.A.D., his meeting and falling in love with Doreen, the horrible realization of the their star-crossed situation, the fatal pack of gum falling on the table, his escape from the office building and how he didn't know how he got here, didn't even know where here was. He drew in a deep breath and sank into silence.

"Why not let him try it?" said Racer. "I was thinking money would be a good reward for his help, but maybe the vaccine would be more valuable to him. After all, none of the rats died from it. The most that happened was that some of them got crabby, not that you can really tell with a rat." The women looked doubtfully at each other and Nelson stared at them with a dawning hope in his eyes.

"Let me try it, I'm begging you. Let me try it, gods knows I've tried everything else. I'll be a lab rat, I'm not proud," he begged. "Really, I'll try anything."

Dr. Linda twisted her hands and tried to come up with a reply. It went against all the protocols, she knew. There should be years more of tests on lab animals to determine its effectiveness and dosage.

"I don't know, I don't know – what if it's not safe? Anything could happen to you," she said. "I don't want to be responsible."

Nelson grabbed her by the arm and put the most pathetic look he could muster on his face. "Anything has been happening to me all week; let me make a decision for myself for a change instead of being bounced around by fate. Pleeeease?" he begged.

Dr. Linda still didn't look happy, but she went upstairs and mixed up a batch and brought it back to him.

She mixed it into a glass of iced tea and handed it to him. "Here you are; I don't know how long it will take until you feel it work, if it works at all." She heard footsteps in the hallway and said, "Quick, out the door! Dr. Cutter's here. He'll have a fit if he sees…"

It was too late, Dr. Cutter was through the doorway and there was no way Nelson could escape. But it didn't matter at all; Dr. Cutter had eyes only for Racer and talked nonstop to him. Racer was too busy eating to make much of a reply, and the two of them went out the door and up the stairs.

Nelson stood numbed. He had convinced himself that he had imagined Racer talking, that it was just a matter of too much stress and not enough sleep that had made him hallucinate. But the sight of the man and hamster in familiar conversation brought the painful reality home.

Yes, there was a talking hamster in the world and he, Nelson had met him and talked to him. He felt behind him for the chair and slowly sank into it.

Weeks went by and life settled down into as normal a routine as you can get in a genetics laboratory. Dr. Cutter bought a bald eagle from Burt, a local poacher, and told him he would pay good money for the largest snapping turtle he could find. Alive and unharmed, they had to be, or they weren't any good. What he really coveted was a member of the local nudist colony, who supposedly had developed the art of invisibility. Everybody talked about them, although an actual sighting was rare. But Burt firmly drew the line at acquiring human subjects; he was crooked, not stupid.

Dr. Linda arrived late at work one Tuesday, wet through and laden down with a chicken pie and containers of chicken corn soup. Traipsing from one mud sale to another, looking for a miniature pig for Dr. Cutter, she was cold and tired. She had a vigorous bidding war for a fine one at the Strasburg Fire Co. but a stranger from D.C. outbid her. She tried to get the license plate number, because there were rumors of a rival lab trying to infiltrate the area.

She entered the locker room and took off her raincoat and shook the rain out of her hair. "It's coming down cats and dogs out there, Helga, and the traffic was backed up from Strasburg to New Providence. I'm glad we're in a quieter part of the county. I wouldn't want to put up with that every day." She turned and looked at Dr. Helga who had her head down and hadn't said a word.

"Helga, is everything all right? Look at me, what's wrong? Helga?"

Dr. Helga raised her head, her face was red from crying and she looked tired down to the bone.

"Hi Linda," she croaked, "I'm just not having a good day, that's all." She reached up and adjusted the brightly colored scarf covering her head and tried to walk around

Dr. Linda to get out of the room. Dr. Linda caught her by the arm and blocked the way.

"Not so fast, Helga, what's going on? When did you start wearing a scarf? I thought the weight loss treatment was going well."

Dr. Helga broke into sobs and sank down on the bench. "It was, it was going so great; I lost fifty pounds in three months, and I was eating like a starved horse. I thought I was in heaven, and then this!" She pulled the scarf off of her head to reveal a completely bald scalp. A very healthy scalp, mind you, but still, quite bald.

"Last night I was brushing my hair and it all fell out. It didn't hurt or anything like that. I felt little twitches all over my scalp and the hair just dropped. It almost felt like it was being thrown out. Oh, what am I going to do? I just bought all new clothes to show off my new figure and then this had to happen! Will my hair grow back? Will I be bald for life? I've been sick all night worrying about it, and chewing my nails to the quick." She held up her fingers to show the wear and tear they'd suffered during the long night.

"Oh my gods," moaned Dr. Linda, stuffing her fist into her mouth to stifle the sound. "Oh, I knew it was too easy, too good to be true. Your figure looks great, but what a price to pay. What are we going to do? Maybe Dr. Cutter…"

Dr. Helga cut her off quickly. "Not a word to him, do you hear? He's not going to help, and if he's in a bad mood, he'll fire both of us, maybe Lefter, too. No, we'll have to figure something out ourselves; I'll wear a scarf and tell the others it's a new fad. Dr. Cutter won't care, he probably won't even notice." She frowned in thought and tried to think where the skinny mixture had gone so wrong. Lefter had a healthy head of hair, so it didn't look like it would come from him.

She reached up and scratched her head as she thought; and after a while she noticed she was still scratching her head. What was that all about? It felt like something was inside her head and wanted out.

"Yes, we do want out, we've had our fun," a voice inside her head said. "After all, you can't do anything more to us, we're dead. Ha ha ha ha ha!"

Dr. Helga shrieked and jumped up on the couch. "Rats! Rats! They're in my head, get them out! Get them out! Make them go away. Oh, what did I do to deserve this?" she cried.

Dr. Linda stared at her friend in horror. Oh, no, the rats have gotten to her, too. She grabbed Dr. Helga and held her tight until she stopped shaking.

"Hold on, Helga, they'll go away in a minute." I hope so, she thought to herself. She checked carefully inside her own skull, no, didn't seem to be any one there but herself; just a faint mocking laughter that died away.

"Oh, they're gone now. I'm alone in my head again, what a wonderful feeling! Linda, there were rats in my head, I mean, not real rats, I mean… I mean… I don't know what I mean. Like shadows or echoes or something. Am I going crazy Linda?" she pleaded to her friend.

"Only if I'm going crazy too, Helga. They were in my head a few weeks ago; they said they were ghosts of the lab rats we used. First that radiation leak up-river from us, and now this. The world seems to get crazier and more dangerous every day. Come on, we're due in the lab now. We'll sneak in quietly while Dr. Cutter has his face in a microscope."

They tidied themselves up, put on a mask of bored indifference and entered the lab. Dr. Cutter indeed had his nose to the grindstone and didn't notice them at all. The two women went through the motions of work, but their minds were far away.

Chapter 12

More weeks went by and Dr. Helga's hair slowly started growing back, but as the hair came back, so did most of the weight.

"Linda, it's just not fair!" cried Dr. Helga to her friend. "All that work, all that suffering I went through, and here I am almost back to my old weight. Do you think we should spend any more time on this skinny vaccine?"

"I think we tried it on humans too early. It needs a lot more animal testing. After all, none of the hamsters lost any hair. And look at poor Nelson, the nicotine vaccine helped him quit, but those big purple spots all over him are just horrible, and they aren't going away. What a fiasco this has all been! Maybe we should give up our experiments for a while," she sighed.

Dr. Linda and Dr. Helga looked at each other in despair and resignation, but they both knew they would keep working on their goals.

Rain poured down on Park Avenue and on the lone figure huddled in his trench coat outside the American

Lung Association headquarters. Nelson was hoping for a glimpse of Doreen as she headed home.

He longed to talk to her, but didn't know if he dared. The vaccine had worked wonderfully well in some ways; he wasn't smoking anymore, and didn't have any cravings either. On the other hand, the large purple spots all over him were hard to disguise. Even in the 'I've-seen-it-all' attitude of New Yorkers, he turned heads everywhere he went. Cab drivers wouldn't stop for him, panhandlers crossed the street when they saw him and in the subway he cleared a car of people in ten seconds flat.

That was two months ago, his savings were nearly gone and he was living in a lesser-known region of the subway tunnels. Even that was uncertain, the regular homeless people and rats were looking at him funny, muttering and threatening to throw him out. He needed a job and how could he get one with those spots staring everybody in the face? Lost in thought, he didn't see the figure approaching him.

"Nelson? Is that you? I thought so." Doreen took his arm and pulled him out of the shadows and down the street. "I was worried sick about you," she said softly. "I didn't hear from you for so long... My gods, what happened to your face? Are you all right? Well, I mean, you can't be, looking like that, but where have you been? You look a wreck."

Nelson looked down at her and struggled to speak "T.O.A.D.," he croaked. "Got fired, met a doctor, new vaccine, h... h... hamster..." he trailed off.

Speech, the shiny sword of every lawyer was but a broken reed to him in this, his hour of need. How could he tell Doreen about everything he had experienced since he had last seen her? Especially the hallucinations; he shuddered at the mere thought of Racer and hoped desperately he would never see another hamster in his life.

But Doreen was here, talking to him, looking compassionately at him, perhaps there was still hope in this upside-down world. He took her hand in his and poured out his heart to her as every lover since the beginning of time has done. He told about all his hopes, dreams, his plans and how they were all impossible and meaningless without her.

Doreen listened with a quiet concentration to his string of adventures, knowing quite well that there was something he wasn't telling her. Well, no matter, it would come with time.

She took his arm and said, "Come home with me, Nelson, some chamomile tea is just what you need. There's nothing so bad that a good cup of herbal tea won't take the edge off it."

After everything Nelson had gone through lately, the thought of drinking herbal tea seemed rational and sane, even desirable; at least you know where you are with a cup of tea. The darkness cast a gentle cloak over them as they made their way down the street, two people who had found each other, after all their trials. Fate, seeing that his goal was accomplished with these two, popped into a coffee shop for a latte and put his feet up for a well-deserved rest.

Chapter 13

It was race day in Pennsylvania, the sky was clear and a fresh breeze skipped happily over the racetrack. Happily, because the wind liked races as much as people do. Any excuse to go fast, make lots of noise and disturb the neighbors. The stands were packed, there were people crammed onto the stairways and more people streaming in the front gates. A bold, bright banner announced the event inside:

R.A.S.C.A.R.
The Rational Association of Stock Car Racing
America's new sport of kings!

Several teams formed in the short time since it had started, complete with corporate sponsors, team uniforms, team egos and flashy, expensive cars. America had found a new love affair and the honeymoon was on.

Percy Bumblebaum sat next to Dr. Cutter in the VIP lounge and drew contentedly on a fat cigar. Usually, out of habitual caution and secrecy, he would avoid being seen in public, but today he didn't care, he was too happy to be careful.

"Look at that crowd," he crowed to Dr. Cutter. "It's a sack full of gold every race day. The public can't get enough of it; it's a money tree, just like you said you could make. With your cut, you can build any kind of lab you want, hire anybody you want. It's a win-win for everybody, my boss is happy, the public loves it and you make out all right, too."

Dr. Cutter liked the sound of money, but it bothered him that he couldn't remember talking to Percy about the Zoomer Juice. What had he said to him? What deal did they make? It was frightening; it was almost like there was another Dr. Cutter out there doing things behind his back. Like that interview with *Mad Scientists Monthly* that he didn't remember giving; he couldn't believe his eyes when that showed up in his mailbox.

He wanted to ask Racer about it, but he didn't like showing a weak front to even his closest friend. Well, he would have to think about it later; right now he was determined to put it out of his mind and enjoy the day.

Down in the stands another group was enjoying the day. Lefter, with Racer in his shirt pocket was there. Dr. Linda, Dr. Helga, Nelson and Doreen were there, grinning broadly and cheering their favorites on.

"Come on, Dave," yelled Lefter.

"Give 'em heck!!" added Racer. He wasn't sure what heck was, but he knew it was something that humans gave each other on a regular basis. Must be something good, he figured.

Dr. Linda and Dr. Helga grinned and waved colorful pennants while sharing a tub of popcorn and a jumbo drink in the welcome sun. Although Dr. Helga's hair had grown back nicely and her weight was slowly dropping, she wasn't ready to take a chance with more of that skinny vaccine. They were just going to have to go back to the drawing board on that one and try something else.

They had invited the newly married couple, Nelson and Doreen, for a day in the country and to meet their friend Dave in person. Doreen treated Nelson's spots with chamomile tea and organic parsnip plasters and the spots finally gave up, packed their bags and left. Now Nelson could face the public again and was able to talk to people without cringing. His new job with the American Lung Association bolstered his sagging spirits to the point he didn't need to see Dr. Tell-Me-Everything anymore, much to that doctor's dismay. The doctor had three more years of boat payments to make, and with Nelson, he had calculated he could even move up to a bigger boat. What a loss to the medical world, the doctor sighed to himself.

Fate too, was in the stands, smiling down on the scene. He could smell a whole new world of opportunity to meddle in people's lives and he couldn't wait to see what trouble he could make with this new sport.

Dave was now a famous figure in the sports world and he couldn't wipe the big, ear-to-ear grin off of his face. His job was a dream come true for him, and he couldn't imagine doing anything else. He came back to the lab every so often to visit the staff and have a cup of coffee. He had a feeling; he couldn't say why, that the lab's coffee was good luck for him. Just one of those things, he mused.

"Order! Order! You're both out of order! Sit down and shut up both of you!" Otto banged one of his leathery leaves on the windowsill to make himself heard, but it didn't have the effect he wanted; not like on TV, when the judge bangs his gavel and everyone gives him their respectful attention. Otto liked to watch TV and he loved courtroom scenes. I wonder if I can grow myself a gavel, he pondered. After all it's made out of wood and I can make cellulose, so it shouldn't be too hard; I'll put it on my to-do list. The black silk robes were going to be a little harder to do.

"He started it!" Squeaker protested. "Accusing me of attempted murder! I just wanted to play with him, that's all. He's got no sense of humor."

"Humor! You call that humor? He tried to kill me, Otto. I have witnesses! Those new hamsters saw it all. They'd tell you about it if they weren't too traumatized. They were so upset, they ate to cope with the stress and it threw off Dr. Helga's experiment with the skinny vaccine. Interfering with work, it's outrageous! We hamsters are proud to do our part in the advancement of medicine and how are we to do it with this monster on the loose?"

"Now, now Racer, we're all monsters, aren't we? Or else we wouldn't be here. But I see your point; we need to work something out. If the lab doesn't succeed, we don't have a home."

"Now Squeaker, what would it take to get you to leave Racer alone? Attention? What do you mean attention? Petting? You like it when humans touch you? Well, it takes all kinds, I guess. Okay, here's what I propose…"

Rain lashed the windows of Plastic Genetics, exploring every crack in the building looking for a way in. Lefter and Dr. Linda stood at the window, arms around each other's waist, watching the fading light and pondering their future.

"Oh Lefter, it's so nice to be here together, all safe and warm, but can it stay this way? Is your uncle upset about us being together? He's walking around here looking like he's seeing ghosts," said Linda.

"He's got something on his mind," replied Lefter, "but I don't think it's us. He won't tell me what's bothering him, but I think it's something about that I.R.S. agent who came to see him. I wonder what happened. He keeps looking at Otto out of the corner of his eye and shuddering. But forget about him for a while, we need to go house shopping. I saw a nice little place down between the Shady Rest and the Rat Hole. Let's go look at it when the rain lets up. It's not the best neighborhood, but it has a nice view of the river."

"The Shady Rest? The Rat Hole? I don't understand this town, why do they need two dives, isn't one enough for any place?"

"Well," Lefter considered. "You see, the Rat Hole is a classy dive, where you have to be able to stay on your feet, keep your clothes on and mind your manners. The Shady Rest is a quiet place where people can let their hair down and you can take your pet rat down for a beer. I can't figure it out, but they won't let rats in the Rat Hole. Not that they aren't there anyway. But it's the cheap part of town and we can get a starter home there."

Dr. Linda sighed happily and squeezed him tighter. "It's a new start for both of us, Lefter. We can build a home together and with the profit sharing we get from the Zoomer Juice we can even get a toaster!" They grinned at each and giggled at the life of luxury awaiting them.

On the counter behind them Racer rearranged his fresh bedding into a proper nest on the floor, and Squeaker stretched in her basket and yawned. They had finally agreed to a truce after Otto had negotiated terms of neutrality. Squeaker agreed not to attack Racer, or even stare in his direction any more, and Racer agreed to try to talk Squeaker up to the humans and get them to pay more attention to her. Fleece's threats had shown them what a perilous ship they sailed in and how quickly it could be sunk.

Down the road, in an empty field, boys on motorbikes and ATVs rode round in circles. Hour after hour, day after day, in rain and heat and dark of night, they rode or watched others ride with a serious silence that they neither questioned nor understood. With a quiet business air of 'a-man-has -to-do-what-a-man-has-to-do' they went at it as a serious job of work that had to be done, a preparation for some distant, unknown test. Did they hope? Did they dream? Shiny cans of Zoomer Juice lay scattered about in the short grass and Fate stood at the edge of the field and nodded his approval.

Racer Quiz

Earn one point for each correct answer.

1. What does R.A.S.C.A.R. stand for?

2. What does T.O.A.D. stand for?

3. Who is T.O.A.D.'s archenemy?

4. What is the Cats' Credo?

5. What night do the hamsters have their glee club?

6. Which fate does the author fear the most?

    A. Invasion by ghost rats
    B. Getting whacked by a tobacco lawyer
    C. That the skinny vaccine will never be discovered
    D. That the boys down the street will never grow up and stop going around in circles with their dirt bikes and making endless noise.
    E. All of the above

7. Where is Plastic Genetics located?

8. What is the blunt instrument that Lefter uses to defend the lab?

9. What skill does Squeaker Cat have that no one knows about?

10. Does Otto believe in evolution or intelligent design?

    A. Evolution
    B. Intelligent design
    C. Both

11. What idea did Racer come up with that brought in the funds needed to build the lab?

12. Why did the U.S. invade Quackii?

13. Where did Dr. Helga come from and why?

14. What is the hamsters' favorite treat?

15. What is Dr. Cutter's dream?

16. Why is Dr. Linda working at PG?

17. What are three things that always be found outside any minit market in the country?

18. What does Squeaker Cat want Dr. Linda to make for her?

19. What made R.A.S.C.A.R. so popular?

20. What did Lefter and Racer contribute to R.A.S.C.A.R.?

21. Who does Percy raise money for?

22. What is T.O.A.D.'s new product?

Quiz Answers

Earn one point for each correct answer.

1. What does RASCAR stand for?
The Rational Association of Stock Car Racing

2. What does T.O.A.D. stand for?
Tobacco Overlords American Division

3. Who is T.O.A.D.'s archenemy?
The American Lung Association

4. What is the cats' credo?
If it doesn't involve tuna, it's not really important.

5. What night do the hamsters have their glee club?
Wednesday

6. Which fate does the author fear the most?
   A. Invasion by ghost rats
   B. Getting whacked by a tobacco lawyer
   C. That the skinny vaccine will never be discovered
   D. That the boys down the street will never grow up and stop going around in circles with their dirt bikes and making endless noise.
   E. All of the above

   E. All of the above

7. Where is Plastic Genetics located?
Lancaster County, PA

8. What is the blunt instrument that Lefter uses to defend the lab?
Stale fasnachts

9. What skill does Squeaker Cat have that no one knows about?
She can answer the phone and imitate Dr. Cutter's voice.

10. Does Otto believe in evolution or intelligent design?
    A. Evolution
    B. Intelligent design
    C. Both

    C. Both

11. What idea did Racer come up with that brought in the funds needed to build the lab?
The Mad Scientist's Starter Kit for Children

12. Why did the U.S. invade Quackii?
No one knows

13. Where did Dr. Helga come from and why?
She came from California to escape a medical inquiry.

14. What is the hamsters' favorite treat?
Whoopee pies

15. What does Dr. Cutter dream of becoming?
An evil world power

16. Why is Dr. Linda working at PG?
Because of the bad national economic situation and she has to support her sick mother

17. What are three things that can always be found outside any minit market in the country?
Loiterers, litterers and an unattended motor vehicle with its engine running

18. What does Squeaker Cat want Dr. Linda to make for her?
A tuna flavored hamster

19. What made R.A.S.C.A.R. so popular?
The addictive Zoomer juice

20. What did Lefter and Racer contribute to R.A.S.C.A.R.?
The left-hand turn gene and the round-and-round gene

21. Who does Percy raise money for?
The U.S. military

22. What is T.O.A.D.'s new product?
Nikki Cheese

0-6 points:	Even the lab hamsters can do better than that.
8-12 points:	You might be able to get a job cleaning up at Plastic Genetics.
14-20 points:	Put on your white lab coat, you could be a scientist.
21-22 points:	You could be a world power!

About the Author

I'm a fifty-something woman who lives under a rock in southern Lancaster County, Pennsylvania. It's OK, I like my rock. Once in a while I peek out to see what all the noise is about and that's where the stories come from.

"I live in Denial, it's a grand place to be,
And I visit Delusion down by the sea."

36575313R00076

Made in the USA
Charleston, SC
09 December 2014